IT'S NEVER A FAIR GAME

JESSICA K. POWELL

COLLEGE BOY
PUBLISHING
"We Breed Bestsellers"

FICTION/URBAN LITERATURE
YOUNG ADULT/AFRICAN AMERICAN

ISBN-13: 978-1-944110-37-6

Edited by **LaTangela Vann** & **Armani Valentino**

for College Boy Publishing

Published for print & digital distribution by **Armani Valentino**
Inside Designed & Setup by **Armani Valentino**

Cover Design by **Armani Valentino**

Published in Dallas, TX, by College Boy Publishing. College Boy Publishing is a division of The College Boy Company & ArmaniValentino.com.

Wholesale copies of this book may be ordered directly from the publisher at www.collegeboypublishing.com. Please allow up to 10-14 Business Days for delivery.

The author is available for keynote addresses, workshops, panel discussions, consultations, and radio & television interviews by emailing collegeboypublishing@gmail.com

Printed in the United States of America

08 09 10 11 12 JPAV 5 4 3 2 1

IT'S NEVER
A FAIR GAME

JESSICA K. POWELL

In loving memory of Gladys Champion.

With lasting love from a world without you, your beautiful soul shall never be forgotten.

This one is for you Grandma.

It's Never A Fair Game

JESSICA K. POWELL

IT'S NEVER
A FAIR GAME

An Urban Street Tale

Chapter One

A MIRACLE IS HERE

She didn't cry when she was born. As a matter of fact she didn't make a sound at all. She just looked around the room and gazed back at all of the amazed faces staring at her. Born at 28 weeks and weighing only three pounds, she was the size of a grown man's hands. Every nurse in the room stood with their mouth wide open, staring in amazement at this tiny yet seemingly healthy baby. She was alert, quiet, and calm. She beat the odds, and survived the harsh conditions her mother had put her in while being pregnant. Although she was severely strung out on crack, the mother had somehow delivered a healthy baby. "What a miracle!"

"I can't believe she's doing so well. I mean, considering the fact that her mother ingested cocaine while on her way to the hospital to give birth," said Dr. Hendrix.

Nurse Tammy shook her head in disbelief... "That's horrible. That baby definitely had God watching over her because her mother sure as hell wasn't."

Dr. Hendrix nodded her head in agreement. "The worst part is that her mother is still so high from the drugs that she refuses to see or name the baby," Tammy continued.

Dr. Hendrix got up with a very stern and concerned look on her face. "I will go speak with the mother myself," she said.

"Hello, Ms. Johnson. My name is Dr. Hendrix. I delivered your baby today. I know you

It's Never A Fair Game

don't remember much because you blacked out during the delivery, but I need to talk to you about your health and the risk you put the baby in. Ms. Johnson, I'm very aware that you abuse drugs, and that you actually used on your way to the hospital to give birth today. Do you mind telling me why?"

Ms. Johnson opened her eyes and gave the doctor an unapologetic look and said, "Because I wanted to get high, that's why. Look here, doc, I know you're just doing your job by being concerned and all, but what I do in the streets is my own fucking business."

"Ms. Johnson, what you do while carrying an unborn child is very much my business. And frankly, in my honest opinion, you're in no shape to raise a child. You were very lucky today. Somehow, you managed to have a healthy baby. She is premature but otherwise as healthy as a full-term baby who wasn't exposed to drugs," said Dr. Hendrix.

"Well, thank you, doc. Thank you for doing ya job like you were supposed to and delivering me a healthy baby." Ms. Johnson's eyes rolled, and she gave a little sarcastic look.

"Oh, you don't need to be thanking me, Ms. Johnson. You need to thank the Lord. As a matter of fact, you will not want to thank me at all

CHAPTER ONE—A Miracle Is Here

once I make my recommendation to remove the child from your custody," said Dr. Hendrix angrily.

"Lady, I don't give a damn what you do. Nobody's going to want that baby, and she'll be right back with me, her mama. So you go right ahead and do whatever you wanna do. As a matter of fact, you can even name the little bastard," laughed Ms. Johnson.

Dr. Hendrix got up and exited the room. As she walked down the hall, she decided to take a trip to the nursery. As she entered the nursery, her heart was heavy. The sound of crying babies echoed off the walls. There were a couple of other mothers inside holding their babies. Dr. Hendrix gave them a smile and continued to make her way straight to the bed that read, *Johnson Girl.* She was so tiny that her attachments for oxygen almost covered her entire face. As she looked at the baby, she couldn't imagine someone so small and so innocent being born to such an undeserving mother.

She held the baby up to her chest and whispered, "You will be loved little one. Someday someone will give you all the love you truly deserve." As she pulled the baby down from her chest, she saw a smile and the cutest dimple appear on the baby's face. This made Dr. Hendrix

It's Never A Fair Game

smile in return. Then it dawned on her that Baby Johnson was the only baby currently in the nursery with no name. Being that Ms. Johnson had given her permission to name the baby, the doctor took a deep breath and looked at the baby and said, "I can't let you be the only nameless baby in here, now can I? After all, you've been through today, I think you should be called Miracle. Yes, Little Miss Miracle Johnson fits you perfectly." Dr. Hendrix walked over to the name sign on her bed and wrote Miracle on it.

As the next few days went by Dr. Hendrix began going by the nursery daily and sometimes twice a day. She knew it would be a mistake to form any attachment to a newborn baby that had yet to even bond with its mother but she didn't care. She liked spending any free moments she had during her busy day with Miracle. It made her feel like the mother she had always wanted to be.

Weeks passed, and Miracle was doing amazingly well. Her weight was up to five pounds, and Dr. Hendrix knew that it was only a matter of time before Miracle would be released from the hospital and into foster care. The very thought of this saddened her. Although she cared about Miracle as if she was her own, she herself was not married, lived a very busy life as

CHAPTER ONE—A Miracle Is Here

a doctor, and could not care for Miracle with in the manner in which she deserved. So the thought of adopting her never stayed in her mind for long.

After she'd been in the hospital for a month, it was time for Miracle to be released. Dr. Hendrix went to the nursery to see Miracle one last time. "Well, hello little one," said Dr. Hendrix. "My, where has the time gone? You've gotten big on me."

Miracle looked up at the doctor as if she knew her voice and smiled.

"It looks like the time has come for you to leave us, little Miracle. I'm going to miss seeing you every day, little one. You have been my reason for taking a new route on my daily rounds, just to come to hold you and talk to you." Dr. Hendrix chuckled while holding Miracle. "But now I have to let you go, my dear. I have to let you live up to the name I gave you. It was a miracle that you lived and you will continue to live and strive through every obstacle you may face in life."

Dr. Hendrix kissed Miracle, held her up to her chest, and whispered to her, "You are loved, Miracle Johnson, and don't you ever forget it." With tears in her eyes, the doctor put Miracle back in her bed and walked away. The next day

It's Never A Fair Game

Miracle was released to foster care.

Babies don't know the difference between being in foster care and being at home with their birth parents. And it was for this reason Miracle was a happy baby. She was very playful and friendly, which was not the norm for a crack baby, at all. She didn't suffer from symptoms of withdrawals nor did she cry from the sound of loud noises. She was a healthy baby in every way.

Over the months her mother, Ms. Johnson, had been taking the necessary steps to get clean and win back custody of Miracle. She would visit with her at least four times a week. Her commitment, coupled with passing every random drug test she took seemed to win the court system over. So by the time Miracle turned a year old she was back in the custody of her birth mother. And Ms. Johnson, for the first time since Miracle was born, seemed genuinely happy to have her. She cared for her and worked hard to be a good mother. She found a job at a hotel as a maid. It didn't pay much, but it was enough for her and Miracle to survive. She applied for all of the government assistance available to her and was approved. She had food stamps, free childcare, and a place to stay. Ms. Johnson and Miracle were doing just fine. Life was good.

Chapter Two

ANYTHING FOR JAMES

"Happy Birthday to you. Happy birthday to you. Happy Birthday, dear Miracle. Happy birthday to you. Blow out your candles, baby," said Ms. Johnson. "Today is your thirteenth birthday!" Miracle blew out her candles with one big breath. "Well, did you make a wish, baby?" asked Ms. Johnson.

"Yes, Mama. I did," replied Miracle. "If it's going" to come true, I can't tell you, Mama."

"That's right, baby," laughed Ms. Johnson. "Well, hurry along. You're going to be late for school. James will be here any minute to give me a ride to work."

Miracle just nodded her head and got up to get her stuff together for school. She wasn't too fond of James, the neighborhood drug dealer, but her mother loved him. Even at thirteen years old, Miracle knew that no good would come from her mother dating a street guy like James. She worried about this every day. As Miracle was walking out the door to head to school, James arrived and honked the horn. "Come on now, Loretta, I got shit to do," he yelled.

Ms. Johnson came running out the door and got into the car. "Well, hey to you too, James. What's wrong with you this morning?" asked Loretta.

"Man, my bad for yelling, boo, I just got a lot of shit to handle after I drop you off today."

"Shit like what?" asked Loretta.

It's Never A Fair Game

"Like Five-O has been watching me type shit. I got to move my product around a bit. Can't have them raiding my spots and just taking all I've worked hard for like that. Ya feel me?"

"Yes, James. But I wish you could get out of the game. You know, like save up enough money and me, you and Miracle go have a great life somewhere."

"Loretta, you know good and damn well I can't just run off and live happily ever after somewhere. The streets is my life, baby. They raised me, and now they need me. And ain't nobody else out here pushing the amount of weight I'm pushing and delivering the same quality product as me. I'm the king out here in these streets. And "ain't" no bitch gon' make me leave that alone."

Loretta just gazed tearfully out the window. As much as she loved James and wished that he could be the man she needed for her and Miracle, she knew he would never be that.

Later that night, after Miracle went to bed, Loretta invited James over. As soon as James got there, he was greeted by Loretta, half-naked with see-through black lace lingerie on. She motioned for him to come into her bedroom, and when he entered he closed the door behind them.

CHAPTER TWO—Anything for James

Loretta could tell that James was high and she seduced him. She lightly pushed him on the bed and started unbuckling his belt and unzipping his jeans. James just grinned like he knew what was in store for him.

Loretta proceeded to take off his pants, moving very slowly and seductively. Once his pants were completely off, she grabbed his dick with her hands and said, "Now close your eyes and let your boo take you away from all of your troubles, baby." She put James' penis in her mouth, and he suddenly felt his blood rushing through his veins. It felt as if he was getting a massage by her throat. With his eyes rolling back in his head, he felt paralyzed from the rhythmic suction of her luscious lips and moist tongue. He enjoyed every minute of this unexpected pleasure.

After she pleased James, she looked at him and said, "James, if you won't leave the streets for me, then can I at least be your partner? Can I help you and be a part of what you're trying to build, James?"

James seriously stared at her "Loretta, this is life or death. The business I'm in is dangerous. It's not for suckas. You have a child to look after. If anything happens to you or we get busted, then what happens to Miracle? These

It's Never A Fair Game

are all the questions you need to ask yourself before you try to get down with me as far as business is concerned." "Nah, Loretta this ain't for you," said James. "I just feel like mixing business with pleasure is never a smart business move."

"But James I promise I will only help your business grow, not hurt it."

"Look here now Loretta, my money comes first, and when people cross me, or they interfere with my business or my money, they get dealt with. Now a nigga care about you and all, but if I let you in and you cross me, Loretta you will be dealt with just like everyone else. So think long and hard woman. Is this what you want?"

Loretta just sat there and quietly stared at James as if she was thinking and weighing her options. Then, after a few quiet minutes, she said, "Ok, I thought about it. And I want in. You let me worry about my child. I got this."

James shrugged and said, "Okay."

They finished making love and went to sleep. Loretta slept peacefully that night. She knew this would be the way to get closer to James and ultimately win his heart.

James seemed to have it all figured out. Loretta would be a part of his inside drug opera-

CHAPTER TWO—Anything for James

tion. She would sell to his business clients. He would have Loretta selling his product out of the rooms she cleaned at the hotel where she worked. You see, Loretta cleaned the third and fourth-floor rooms all by herself.

So when James would have clients in town visiting who needed a fix, he would have them stay at the hotel where Loretta worked and have them request to stay in a room on the third or fourth floor. They would check into their room and leave the money under the bed. Loretta would enter the room, retrieve the money and leave the product. She wrote in the guest log that she delivered fresh towels in case someone asked why she was entering the rooms at odd times. They had a plan.

Loretta knew that James was already on the feds' radar for his drug business, but she didn't care. She wanted to be a part of him and what he had going on in any way possible. So for the next few months, she carefully made secret drug trades in the hotel rooms of her workplace. For a while, things were going according to plan.

Then one day Loretta got a call from her boss on her day off. He was calling to inform her that he was going to be cutting hours. Business had been pretty slow, and he didn't need as many housekeepers for a while.

It's Never A Fair Game

Hearing this made Loretta nervous. She feared what might happen if someone else was working her floors for the next few weeks or months maybe. Yeah, James could put the word out to his clients that she wouldn't be there for a few weeks but what if someone forgot or didn't get the memo and checked in on the third and fourth floors trying to score some dope? Loretta didn't want to risk losing her main job trying to help James.

Immediately she called James and asked him to come by that night to discuss something important. Loretta knew better than to talk about anything that had to do with the drug business on the phone or in front of Miracle. She wanted to keep this part of her life as far away from Miracle as she could. She had already lost her to the system one time and made a promise to herself as well as Miracle that she would never let that happen again. But Miracle was mature beyond her years, and she knew something was different with her mother these days. And she had a feeling that whatever was going on, it had something to do with James.

Later that night when James arrived, Loretta seemed a bit hesitant to tell him about the unexpected change that would be taking place at her job.

CHAPTER TWO—Anything for James

"So what did u call me over for tonight, Loretta? Am I about to get some more of that unexpected loving again?" grinned James.

"Nah boo, it's not that," replied Loretta.

"Well, what is it?"

"Well, James, my boss called me today."

"Ok, and?"

"Well, James, he said that the hotel has been kind of slow lately and that he would be cutting hours, meaning mine. So in other words, while I'm at home someone else will be working my floors!"

James looked at her like he was already thinking of his next move. "It's all good, Loretta. I'll put the word out to my clients. I'll come up with a way to make sure this works for everybody, including you."

"James, I just want to make sure if anything happens I will be ok, and that Miracle will be ok," said Loretta.

With a stern face, James looked at Loretta and said, "As long as I'm good then you and Miracle are good, and that's my word."

Knowing this seemed to ease Loretta's mind. She smiled at James and hugged him. He was the sense of security she always wanted and needed for her and Miracle. And even though she knew with his lifestyle that each day

It's Never A Fair Game

could be the day he got caught or killed in the streets, she was determined to spend every moment she could loving him.

Later that day, when Miracle returned from school, she was shocked to see James already at her house and her mother already home from work. When she walked in she was greeted by both her mother and James. She spoke to them both and headed straight to her room to start on her homework. Miracle avoided James as much as she could. In her mind, he wasn't good for her mother, so she kept her words short with James. James, on the other hand, tried, to get Miracle to like him. He had a son by another woman who he rarely got to see because of his lifestyle, so to him, Miracle was like a second chance at being a dad.

Loretta walked into the room to talk to Miracle. "Hey, baby. What you doing?" asked Loretta.

"Nothing Mama. About to start on some homework."

"Baby, can I ask you something? Why don't you like James?"

Miracle looked up at her mother and said, "It's not that I don't like him, Mama, it's just that I don't like him for you."

"What do you mean by that?" asked Loretta.

CHAPTER TWO—Anything for James

"Well, Mama, James sells drugs. I don't want anything to happen to you. You're all I have, Mama."

Loretta was sad to hear this. She loved Miracle and James and couldn't see herself without either of them. And although her daughter should come first, she could never leave James. She looked at Miracle and said, "I know you may not like him, baby, but you're gonna have to learn to like him because he's not going anywhere no time soon. I want you to have a father, and he's the one I love, so therefore he's gonna have to do."

"But Mama, what if he brings you down with him and his lifestyle? Or what if.." Miracle stopped herself dead in the middle of her sentence, second-guessing if she should say what she was thinking.

"What if what?" asked Loretta, seeming to get angry.

"Well, what if you get tempted by the stuff James always brings around and start back using it yourself, Mama? I don't want you to get like that again." Miracle's eyes started to water as the thought of her mother being on drugs rushed through her mind. The thought of seeing her mother like she had heard she was when she was first born was a scary thought and some-

It's Never A Fair Game

thing that she didn't ever want to become a reality. As far as Miracle was concerned, James being around would only lead to trouble for her mother. Loretta looked at Miracle deeply, as if she didn't know how to respond to Miracle's concerns.

"Miracle, I love you, baby, and I would never go back to being the person that I was when I had you. I worked hard to get myself clean and win custody of you; I'm damn sure not going to do anything to lose you again," said Loretta. She leaned in to hug Miracle and kissed her forehead softly. "Now Miracle baby, will you try to be a little friendlier to James? Can you do it for your mama?" asked Loretta.

"Yes ma'am," replied Miracle. Although she agreed to try, Miracle could never fully trust James or let him be this "father figure" that Loretta wanted him to be for her. Miracle just prayed that one day her mother could see what she saw, a disaster waiting to happen.

As the weeks went by Loretta was still not back to her regular working schedule. James had been helping Loretta pay the bills since the hotel cut her hours. And James paying bills meant he was hanging around the house more than usual. It was almost as if he had moved in. He was there every day now, not like his usual

CHAPTER TWO—Anything for James

two or three times a week visits. Loretta was loving every minute of having her man around, him and his product.

Miracle, on the other hand, felt all alone. Her mother was all she had. And with James around more her bond with her mother felt like it was quickly fading away. Her mother seemed different lately. Miracle couldn't quite put her finger on the change, but she knew something wasn't right about Loretta.

One day Miracle came home from school and Loretta was not in the living room to greet her as usual. "Mama! Mama! Where are you?" yelled Miracle. Miracle walked around the house looking frantically for Loretta. She went to Loretta's bedroom to find her lying on the floor passed out. She walked over to her body and touched her, and she felt warm. Miracle shook Loretta until she woke up. "Mama! Wake up. Why are you lying on the floor? What's wrong, Mama?"

Loretta looked up at Miracle with her eyes rolling in the back of her head and said, "I'm fine, baby. I just needed a nap." She passed back out.

Miracle was pretty sure that whatever was going on with her mother had nothing to do with needing a nap. She began to look around the room in search of an explanation as to why

It's Never A Fair Game

she came home and found her mother passed out on the floor. And she was faced with her worst fear when she walked into the bathroom.

On the sink, Miracle found a mirror with a white substance on it. Miracle knew immediately what the unknown substance was and why her mother was lying on the floor. She was high. She had been using.

Now everything had made sense about her mother's strange behavior in the past few weeks. Miracle knew where her mother got the drugs. The only thing she didn't know was whether or not James had given them to her. In a way Miracle hoped he had given her mother permission to use his product; otherwise, all hell could and would break loose. James was the type of man who was all about his money. If you messed with his money, then there would be hell to pay.

Miracle was worried about what he would do if he found out. So she quickly devised a plan to keep her mother safe just in case he hadn't told her she could use them. She would tell James that she found the drugs, didn't know what they were and threw a little bit away while cleaning her mom's room. Now this plan in no way would stop James from being mad about the loss, but in her mind, it would keep Loretta

CHAPTER TWO—Anything for James

from getting a beat down. And she would sacrifice her safety for her mother's.

A few hours later Loretta woke up to find Miracle sitting on the floor just staring at her. "Mama, I didn't think you would ever get up. Why did you do it, Mama? Why did you take those drugs? What were you thinking, Mama?"

Loretta jumped up without answering one single question Miracle had asked. "Miracle, you need to learn how to stay in a child's place dammit!" she scolded. "I'm grown and can do whatever the hell I want to and whenever the hell I feel like it."

"But Mama, you said that you would never go down that path again! Mama, you said you didn't want to lose me again," cried a tearful Miracle.

"Miracle, you're just a child. You have no idea what the pressures of life will lead you to do. I fought the temptation for so long, baby. I really did. And after a while, my mind got the best of me, and I gave in. I have been sneaking pieces of James' product that he leaves over here for a while, hoping he won't notice. I've been careful, baby, so there is no need to be afraid," said Loretta. "It's going to be alright. And I meant what I said. I don't want to lose you, and I'm not going to lose you. I promise, baby."

It's Never A Fair Game

Miracle hugged her mother. She knew that her mother's safety was in jeopardy. There was no way of knowing how much product her mother had taken from James and just how long she had been taking it. Miracle now feared that her original plan to save her mother would not work. Once again she felt alone. She was losing more and more of her mother by the day, minute and hour. She felt like she lost her first to James, and now to the drugs.

That night Miracle lay in bed awake. The fear of what James would do when he found out her mother had been stealing from him over-whelmed her. And as the days went by Loretta just kept on using. She had even lost her job due to not showing up on the days she was sched-uled to work. The little income she had coming in was now gone. And Miracle knew it was only a matter of time before James started asking questions and everything would come to a head.

In the meantime, Miracle continued to go to school every day and tried to put the stresses of her home life behind her while out of the house. It was the only time her mind felt free, if only for a second. School was fun for her be-cause Miracle loved to learn. She loved to read and often sat and visualized her future and how different her life would be when she grew up.

CHAPTER TWO—Anything for James

The life she envisioned for herself was happy and healthy and didn't have drugs or poverty anywhere in it. She wanted better for herself and worked hard at school so her future could be bright. And now her strung-out mother didn't even care if she went to school or not.

Loretta became so strung out on the drugs Miracle was forced to take care of herself. She started taking Loretta's food stamp card out of her purse and walking to the corner store to get food to cook. She was getting the meals and preparing them. She was running the household at 13 years old, and her mother was on dope. Now being all alone was normal for her. She had gotten used to her mother being passed out and incoherent all the time. To come home and find Loretta passed out in different places all over the house was normal. As long as her mother was breathing and had a heartbeat, Miracle would go to her room and block everything out.

When Loretta would finally wake up, she didn't even remember being passed out at all. The drugs had taken over her life so much that she hadn't even noticed that James hadn't been over to the house in a month. He had gotten locked up for a petty crime. Miracle had heard in the streets that he was locked up, but she chose not to mention it to her mother. She feared what

It's Never A Fair Game

would happen to her mother when he got out.

She knew her house would be the first place he came. He would collect his product from Loretta to get back on the streets and try to make up for some of the money he had lost while being locked up. Miracle hoped that whenever that day came, she would be home to try and help her mother against James. She knew it would go down whenever that day came. She had been mentally preparing herself for the worst, since the first day she caught her mom using.

Chapter Three

GOODBYE MAMA

Miracle awakened to the sound of the doorbell ringing. She got up and headed toward the front door. The closer she got to the door the more curious she became as to who could be ringing the doorbell so early in the morning. The moment she looked through the peephole all of her worst nightmares came true. James was on the other side of the door. For a split second, she thought that maybe if she didn't answer he would get tired of waiting and go away. But the longer she took to answer, the more impatient James grew and began to knock as well as ring the doorbell.

She felt defeated before the war had even started. At this point not opening the door was only making James angry even before he found out what had been going on while he had been away. She definitely didn't want to make things worse. So Miracle took a deep breath and opened the door.

"Hey hey James," she stuttered. "You looking for Mama?"

"Yeah, baby girl, where she at? And what in the hell took y'all so long to answer the damn door? Shit... y'all know a nigga hot out here in these streets."

"I'm sorry, James. I was in the bathroom, and Mama is still asleep."

"Sleep?" asked James. "What in the hell is your mama doing sleep? She supposed to be

It's Never A Fair Game

getting ready to head to work around this time."

"I don't know James. Maybe she's off today," said Miracle.

"Well, don't worry about it, baby girl. I'll find out what's going on." James walked into the house and headed straight to Loretta's room. The dreaded day Miracle knew would come had arrived. She went into her room and closed the door behind her.

James walked into Loretta's room to find Loretta sprawled across her bed sleeping soundly. He didn't want to disturb her, so he decided that he would collect the stash. He counted the product.

James went in the top of the closet in Loretta's room to retrieve his hidden stash, only to look and not see it where he left it. He decided to check a few more places in her room before waking up Loretta. After a few more failed attempts he decided to wake Loretta up and make his presence known.

"Loretta! Loretta, wake up, baby; it's me, James."

"James?" She opened her eyes and smiled at him. She missed him. Well, when she wasn't high on his supply, she did. "Hey, baby. Where have you been all these weeks?" asked Loretta.

"They locked me up for driving with a sus-

CHAPTER THREE—Goodbye Mama

pended license. I tried calling you, but your phone is off. Why is the phone off?" asked James.

"I got fired, James. I didn't have the money to pay the bill."

"Damn, I'm sorry, baby," he said. "I should've been here for you like I told you I would. Don't worry I'ma get the phone cut back on for you, ASAP. I just gotta get out to these streets and put in some work. I lost out on a lot of money while I was away. None of my people could re-up with the connect to get the product because my connect deals with me and only me. The streets been dry out there while I was away. That's why I gotta take my stash and get it to my crew so they can start making this money while I wait on this connect to meet up with me for the re-up."

Immediately she thought about James's stash and how she had been using it to get high. She wasn't ready for James to know what she had done. She had missed him. She loved him. And if only for a moment, she wanted to love on him. Loretta got up and straddled James's lap.

"Baby, you've been gone for over four weeks. I know business is important, but I've been missing you and him." Loretta looked down at James's penis as the "him" she was referring to. James smiled.

It's Never A Fair Game

"Well, why don't you show me how much you've been missing me then, woman," he said.

Loretta started kissing James passionately on the lips. She pulled off his shirt then proceeded to slide her tongue gently down the middle of his chest, slowly making her way down to his pants. James laid back and allowed Loretta to have her way with him. She unbuckled James's belt and unzipped his zipper. She could see that he'd been missing her as well from the way his penis jumped up immediately through the boxer hole. She took his boxers off and gently sat on top of him and proceeded to ride him like a surfboard.

Miracle could hear the moans coming from her mother's room. She was surprised to hear moans and not fussing and arguing. Maybe James took the news of her mother using the drugs pretty well, she thought. All she knew was that she could finally breathe. It felt like since the moment she opened the door and let him in, she had been holding her breath, not knowing what was about to happen next. Miracle decided to go to the store to get a few things for breakfast while her mother and James continued their moaning. She quietly went to the kitchen, grabbed her mother's food stamp card out of her purse and left for the store.

CHAPTER THREE—Goodbye Mama

James and Loretta finished making love and Loretta got up to get a soapy washcloth to clean James off. Once she finished cleaning James off, she went to the bathroom to clean herself as well. James got up and started putting his clothes back on.

"Hey Loretta," he yelled, "I tried looking for my stash while you were asleep and couldn't find it. Did you move it or something?"

"Uh… yes, baby, I moved it to a safer spot for you. Let me finish getting cleaned up, and I'll get it for you, ok?"

"Ok, cool," said James.

Meanwhile, Loretta started to get nervous. She could feel the sweat forming all over her body at just the thought of having to tell him the truth. How do you tell someone that you love you have been stealing from them? She loved James, and she honestly felt like he loved her in return even if he loved the streets a little more. She knew there would be no real way to get herself out of this situation without being completely honest with him and confessing that she now had a drug problem and had been using his product. She took a deep breath and walked back into the bedroom.

"James, we need to talk."

"Ok, so talk," said James.

It's Never A Fair Game

"Well, I need to tell you what's been going on with me while you've been away."

"You told me," he said. "You lost your job."

"Yeah, well, I lost my job for a reason, James."

"Well, what's the reason, Loretta? Aye man, stop beating around the goddamn bush and tell me what the fuck you have to tell me," he snarled.

"James, I been using again," she blurted out.

"Using? Using what?" he asked.

"I've been snorting powder, James. "I've been using your dope that you left here. Baby, I thought I could never go back to it. I thought that part of my life was over. I mean, I have been clean for the last 13 years! With my hours getting cut at work and you not being here, the temptation got the best of me. I'm really sorry, baby. Please don't be mad, James," begged Loretta.

James sat on the edge of the bed, almost in disbelief at what he heard. Without saying a word he stood up and looked at Loretta face to face. Loretta's heart was pounding so loudly with fear she was pretty sure he could hear it through her chest. Without warning, James slapped Loretta to the ground. A tearful and now bloody-lipped Loretta tried to get back up, but

CHAPTER THREE—Goodbye Mama

every time her attempts were unsuccessful due to an angry James knocking her down again. He beat Loretta until she passed out.

When she awoke, she found James standing over her with his pistol in his hand. "Oh please, no! Don't kill me! I promise it will never happen again!"

"Shut up, bitch!" yelled James. "And now you see why a nigga says money over bitches! Because in the end bitches can't be trusted! I thought you was down for a nigga, Loretta. I thought you had my back. I looked out for you and that stuck-up ass child you got, and this is the thanks I get?"

Loretta sat on the floor sobbing and begging for her life. Her eyes were swollen to the point where she could barely even see his face. "I'm sorry, James, just please don't hurt me. Please think about Miracle. I'm all she has. Without me, she has nobody, James, and nowhere to go. Please don't kill me."

"Bitch, your junky ass ain't taking care of her no way. All you've been taking care of is that nose and making sure it's filled with my fucking product!"

"I promise I will pay you back some way, somehow for all that I used, James."

"Oh, I know you will," he said. "You're going

It's Never A Fair Game

to pay me back, or I'm going to kill you, and that's a promise. And since you thought stealing from a nigga that you claimed to love was a good idea, I got an even better idea on how you're going to pay me back."

Loretta, now black-eyed and bruised, looked up at him, more than curious about what he was going to want her to do to pay him back. "Well, what do I have to do?" she asked. "I'm willing to do anything to make things right with us again."

"Well, first off, know there is no us," he said. "You ain't shit to me but a trick. And because all I do with tricks is put them on a corner, that's exactly where I'll be putting your ass. You're gonna get my money back for all the product you stole from me, or I'm going to kill you and trick out your daughter."

Loretta let out a loud cry. "NOOOOOOOO!"

"Don't cry now," he said. "You wasn't crying when you was getting high off my shit! But on another note, I got some good news for you. The good news is I guess you can say you're employed again," he laughed. "But the bad news is that now you work for me, and I'm the worst boss out there. Ain't no days off, bitch. You're gonna make all my money back, and you have your nose to thank for that. Now go get yourself cleaned up and get me the rest of my product so

CHAPTER THREE—Goodbye Mama

I can calculate how much restitution you owe me."

Loretta got up and did as she was told. She never thought James would react this way. Or maybe she was too high to think about the consequences at all. High or sober, Loretta now realized she was wrong in believing he loved her. There was no way that this could be love. Love is not putting your woman on the street to be a hooker to make money for you. And love was not beating your woman until she was black and blue.

James was a thug. And thugs don't love. This was something her 13-year-old daughter had been trying to tell her for the longest, but she hadn't been listening. The only thing that mattered at the time was her love for him and not what anyone else thought or said about it. And now she realized Miracle had been smarter than her and could see right through James. Loretta felt stupid and scared. She was about to enter a street world she had vowed never go back to.

After finishing up in the bathroom, she gave James the rest of his drugs; he concluded that she had stolen around $2500 worth of product from him. He told her that she would trick until she'd paid him back the $2500 she owed plus an extra $2500 for being a

It's Never A Fair Game

disloyal bitch, and he left the house.

Loretta went to Miracle's room to find she was not there but a letter was on the bed. It read: "Hey Mama, I went to the store with your food stamp card to get us some groceries so I can make breakfast. Love, Miracle." Moments after reading the letter she heard the front door open and assumed it was Miracle returning from the store. She went to the front to meet her at the door. Miracle took one look at her mother and instantly realized what happened after she left. "He found out, huh?" she asked her mother.

"No baby. I told him," said Loretta. He didn't take it well. He beat me and said that I'm going to have to pay him back everything that I took, plus extra."

"Well, you don't have a job anymore, Mama. What are you going to do to get him his money back? And what did he say would happen if you didn't get the money, Mama?"

"I don't have the option of not getting it. I have to get it, or I die. That's what he said, baby. And James doesn't play about his money. He said I'll be working for him from now on. So that means you may have some nights at home alone. Please understand, baby. I have to do whatever he says at this point to stay alive. And once I pay him back everything I owe, I will never

CHAPTER THREE—Goodbye Mama

mess with him or a man like him ever again. I should've listened to you when you tried to tell me why I shouldn't love a man like James. And now I must pay the price."

As angry as Miracle felt on the inside toward her mother, feeling sorry for her outweighed the anger. She felt sorry that her mother had got involved with a man like James and that she wasn't strong enough to fight the temptation to take James's drugs.

"Well Mama, maybe I can help you come up with the money," she said. "I can collect cans and find things around the neighborhood to make money."

"NO! I won't have you out here roaming the dangerous streets of Atlanta trying to clean up the mess I made. I will have to do this on my own, baby. And when it's done, it's done."

Miracle hugged her mother tightly. She hated seeing her mother bruised up and broken, and hoped that her mother could write off her debt with James as soon as possible.

About a week later James showed up at the house unannounced. Loretta opened the door and let him in."Hey, baby. Looks like that face is good and healed now," he said. "Tonight will be your first night of work." She had hoped that he had changed his mind about her working for him. He hadn't.

It's Never A Fair Game

Loretta looked uneasy. His mind was made up. Loretta was now his hoe, and he was her pimp.

"Come on now, Loretta, let's have a look in your closet and see if you got anything suitable for your first night of work," he chuckled.

They both went to Loretta's room, and he picked out a dress that he felt was perfect for the night ahead of her. "Go get dressed," he said. "I'll be taking you to work tonight and showing you the ropes."

Loretta did as she was told. James had already put a pistol to her head and threatened to kill her if she didn't get his money back; she knew in order to stay alive she must do everything he said without any objections. Loretta got dressed then asked James if she could go tell Miracle goodbye before she left. James said yes then stepped outside to make a phone call.

Loretta went to Miracle's room. "Miracle baby, I have to start my job working for James tonight," she said.

"Ok, Mama. But be careful and please don't do any more drugs or anything that will make James madder at you," Miracle pleaded.

"I'm not, baby. All I want to do at this point is get this man his money back and get rid of him. Hopefully, he will be locked up for good one day and will never be able to hurt me or threaten our lives again."

CHAPTER THREE—Goodbye Mama

Meanwhile, James had hung up with his phone call and had been walking toward Miracle's room and heard what Loretta said to her. Hearing that Loretta was planning to leave him alone and was secretly hoping that he ended up back in jail pissed him off. But instead of getting angry James decided that Loretta would have to die. She had now become too much of a liability to keep around. She knew what he did for a living, and now she hated him. In his mind, she would sell him out to the cops at any moment to make sure that he got locked up for good.

James wasn't about to let that happen. So he quickly devised a plan to get Loretta before she got him. He went outside to make a phone call. Once he finished, he yelled from the door to Loretta that it was time to go. Loretta kissed her daughter, told her that she loved her and headed out the front door after James.

While riding in the car with James, all she could think about was Miracle. "James, how late do I have to work tonight?" she asked.

"As late as I want you to," he answered.

"James, I know I have to work late nights to get this money back for you, but is there any way you can let me be home a little early some nights? Miracle is home alone, James, and she's only 13 years old. I worry about her, that's all."

It's Never A Fair Game

"Loretta, what you need to worry about is saving your life and making me my money. But I'll tell you what, if you do a good job tonight I'll consider letting you go home to check on her once or twice throughout your shift."

"Oh thank you, James," said Loretta. Although it wasn't what she asked for, she was thankful for something, anything other than a flat-out "NO!".

He pulled over at a side street. "Now look here, Loretta," he said. "I need to give you a run-down of what you need to be charging these niggas out here. And after every dollar you make you need to be running me my money. Ya hear me?"

"Yes James," she answered.

"Blow jobs $50-$100, sex $100-$150, both $150-$200. Always start off with the highest price and work your way down until they agree. You can pretty much look at a nigga and tell if they got big money or not so use your brain," said James.

Loretta paid attention to everything James said. She wanted to do things right, the first time. Once James explained in detail the do's and don'ts of tricking, how to spot police, and pricing, he took her to the corner that he had selected for her to work. It was on the street corner of the

CHAPTER THREE—Goodbye Mama

hotel Loretta had been fired from a few weeks prior. It seemed as if he had selected this spot to degrade and humiliate her ten times more than she was by being a hooker in the first place. As if the beating wasn't enough, Loretta realized that using his drugs was one of the biggest mistakes of her life and now every time she saw James she was paying for it. She wanted to beg him to move her location, but she knew it would only anger him. So instead Loretta just got out of the car and went to the instructed spot without saying a word.

James parked across the street from the hotel and watched her. He watched her every move. If Loretta didn't seem to be applying herself like he felt she should, he would call her cell phone or text her and ask her if she wanted to live. Because she knew James was capable of killing her, Loretta pushed herself to work harder. To stay motivated, she told herself if she worked hard and did a good job James would allow her to check on Miracle. So with each man she stopped and each car she got into, she reminded herself it was for Miracle and did what she had to do.

After about three straight hours of working the corner, Loretta decided to ask James if he was pleased with her performance so far.

It's Never A Fair Game

She was sure she had done well enough to be able to go check on her daughter. She crossed the street and walked over to where James' car was parked.

"James, have I done good tonight? I just want to be able to go check on my baby, James. She's at the house all alone, and you said if I did good then I would be able to check on her."

"Yeah Loretta, that's what I said. And you know what, you have done good. So you pull one more trick and I'll let you go check on her."

Loretta gave out a loud cry of joy. "Oh thank you, James! I promise I'll go pull another trick right now!" She hurried back to her spot on the corner and began trying to get the attention of potential clients. Meanwhile, James made a phone call. Within minutes of the call, a green car pulled up to Loretta, desperate for her services. Loretta hopped in, and the car pulled into a nearby alley.

"So how can I please you tonight, Daddy?" she asked the man. "I'm down for whatever you want."

He looked at Loretta and asked, "Anything?"

"Yeah baby, anything," she repeated.

"Good," he said, "cuz this will be an anything type of night." The man pulled a gun out of

CHAPTER THREE—Goodbye Mama

the back of his shirt and ordered Loretta to get in the back seat. Loretta instantly became over- whelmed with fear and did exactly as she was told. She tried to tell herself that maybe if she stayed calm and just did everything she was told to do, she could survive this attack and still make it home to check on Miracle.

But after the attack went on for an hour, Loretta began to fear the worst. She suddenly realized that she might never see her daughter again. The man had raped her and beat her so badly that she was now losing consciousness. She mustered up the courage and strength to ask the unknown man if he would let her go.

"Please," she begged him, "I have a daugh- ter at home. I promise I won't tell anyone what happened to me if you let me go."

The man looked her in the eyes and said, "Baby, if it was up to me I might, being that no- body would listen to a junky hoe claiming she got raped anyway. But it's not up to me, and the boss man wants you gone. So you gotta go."

Loretta knew instantly who the boss man was. It was James. He had made her believe that if she worked hard tonight, she could go home and check on Miracle. But he knew when she walked out that door that she would never walk back in it again. He had set her up and wanted

It's Never A Fair Game

her dead. Loretta began to scream, hoping that someone walking by or near the alley might hear her screams and save her. But that didn't happen.

The unknown man strangled Loretta in the backseat of the car until she took her last breath. She was dead. After he killed her, he took a rag and wiped down the steering wheel and everything he might have touched in the car. He took the rag, threw it in a nearby dumpster and left the car with a naked Loretta in it. As the man calmly walked away from the crime scene, he phoned James to let him know he had completed the job.

The next morning Miracle awakened to find herself home alone. She walked around the house, looking for any signs that her mother ever came home last night. She concluded that her mother never came home and began calling her cell phone repeatedly. Each time she called was a failed attempt. Loretta was not answering her phone; her mother always answered her phone.

Miracle decided to do something she never thought she would even want to do. She called James in hopes that her mother was with him or that he at least knew where she was. She dialed his number and got a message that the

CHAPTER THREE—Goodbye Mama

person she was trying to reach had a number that was no longer in service. It appeared that he had changed his number. *But why?*

Miracle checked the telephone number and called it again. Once again she received the same automated message. James had changed his telephone number, and her mother was missing. Hours went by and still no Loretta. Miracle had called her phone so many times that the phone was now going straight to voicemail when she called. It appeared that Loretta's phone might be dead. But Miracle was on a relentless search for her mother and didn't care. She called the phone every five or ten minutes and left numerous messages for her mother to call her back as soon as possible.

By night, when she hadn't seen nor heard from her mother all day, she knew something wasn't right. She had an unsettling feeling in the pit of her stomach. Nothing seemed to be adding up. Her mother didn't just vanish into thin air. She knew her mother had problems and didn't always make the best decisions, but she had believed her mother when she said she was going to leave the drugs and her life with James as soon as her debt was paid off. And regardless of where she was, she still believed her.

The whole situation seemed strange.

It's Never A Fair Game

James number had been the same since before he got locked up. So changing his number and not coming by the house to pick up her mama for work made Miracle believe that wherever her mother was, James was too. Or he at least knew where she was. Miracle contemplated whether or not she should call the police. She wanted to know where her mother was by any means necessary, even if that meant getting her in trouble with the law. Her mother had left her alone to go work for a drug dealer. She knew that couldn't be legal. She decided that by tomorrow morning she would call the police if she still hadn't heard from or seen her mother.

The next morning there was still no sign of Loretta. Miracle did the same thing she had done the morning before and walked around the house looking for any clues that her mother might have come home. And once again she didn't find any.

She cut on the TV and sat down to begin calling her mother's phone when suddenly breaking news of an unknown woman's body found in an ally appeared across the television screen. Miracle dropped the phone and gazed at the screen. Her heart fell to the bottom of her stomach. They had not even released the name of the victim, and she had a feeling in her mind,

CHAPTER THREE—Goodbye Mama

body, and soul that it was her mother. Miracle sat on the sofa in silence. Her heart said it was her mother who was found murdered, but her mind wanted to believe that maybe her mother was somewhere alive and this dead woman was not her.

Miracle decided to call the police and report her mother missing. She had no other choice. When Miracle disclosed her age and that she was home alone, they immediately sent a squad car to the residence. The police along with a detective arrived at the house they were accompanied by a detective. Miracle let the police and the detective in to have a look around. Once the detective got a look at the photo of Loretta he gave the other police officer a nod as if confirming the woman found was in fact, Loretta. He asked Miracle to have a seat and then explained to her that her mother was gone.

She cried. Even though she already knew the truth, she cried and cried like the thought of her mother being dead had never even crossed her mind during the time she had been missing. To hear it confirmed seemed unreal. She couldn't imagine living her life without her mother. She was all she had.

It's Never A Fair Game

"Do you have any other relatives you can call to come get you, sweetheart?" asked the detective.

"No sir," she said. "It was just me and my mom. I never met my dad, and I have no other family here. My mama was all I had."

The detective felt heartbroken for Miracle and took her into his arms. He comforted her and told her he would see to it personally that she ended up in a nice home. The thought of having to live in an unfamiliar place made her cry even harder. She couldn't see herself happy anywhere without her mother. The detective walked outside and called Child Services.

Within an hour they were packing Miracle's belongings to take her away. While packing her things she came across a picture she and her mother took when they first moved into the house, they were so happy. Loretta was clean, there was no James, and it was just her and her mom. Miracle put the picture in her bag to have a reminder of her mom before she became an addict again. After a while, the packing was all done, and it was time to go. As Child Protective Services took her away, Miracle watched the house until she could no longer see it.

Chapter Four

A NEW HOME

Because Miracle had no other known relatives, the family court judge put her in foster care. Miracle moved into a group home. They allowed her to attend her mother's small burial. There was no one there but her and the appointed official who brought her. *Where was James, she wondered. James not attending her mother's funeral raised more and more red flags. He had something to do with it. She knew he did. And when she approached her mother's coffin to say goodbye one last time, she made a promise to Loretta that by any means necessary, she would find out who did this to her.*

It took her a long time to get used to being at the group home. For many nights she would wake up in a cold sweat, looking for her mother. It was hard to accept the fact she would never see her again. For many days she spoke to no one and cried in her bed at night. Although she knew every child in the group home must be like her in some way or another, it felt like she was in her situation by herself. She mainly read books to pass the time. It seemed almost easier to read stories about other people's lives than to deal with her own.

Miracle didn't interact with anyone at the home. Her mother had always been the closest person in her life, and no one would ever be able to take her place. And she wasn't trying to let anybody fill that void either. One day she got an

It's Never A Fair Game

unexpected knock on her bedroom door. "Who is it?" she muttered softly.

"It's Mrs. Peterson, the guidance counselor," she answered. "May I come in?"

Miracle opened the door and let her in. "Have I done something wrong?" she asked.

"Oh no, Miracle, I just wanted to talk to you and make sure you're adjusting well and that you're doing ok. That's my job you know," she joked.

"Yes ma'am, I know."

"So how are you doing?" she asked. "How are you adjusting and getting along with the other kids?"

"Ok, I guess," Miracle said.

"What do you mean you guess? Are the other kids treating you ok? Has anyone been bothering you?" asked Mrs. Peterson.

"No, ma'am. I don't really talk to the other kids. I don't have any friends here. My mother was my only friend, and now she's dead." Miracle lowered her head and sobbed.

"Miracle, it will be ok. Has anyone ever told you what happens when you die?" asked Mrs. Peterson.

"You get put inside of a box, and they bury the box in the ground forever," Miracle said.

"Well, that's the part of it that we see, but

CHAPTER FOUR—A New Home

there is, in fact, another part of death we don't get to see. It's called the afterlife."

"What is the afterlife?" Miracle stopped sobbing and held her head up. She wanted to know more about this afterlife.

"The afterlife is the life a person has after death. Your mom's body may be in the ground, Miracle, but her soul lives on. Her soul is up in heaven, sweet child, and she's watching you right now. Whether you know it or not she's with you every day. So you're never alone. You have God, your mother, me and the rest of the staff with you. We are here for you as well."

This was very comforting for Miracle to hear. She needed to hear that her mother was still with her. She decided to remember what Mrs. Peterson said so she could use it in times of need. And whenever she felt down about her mother's passing, she would replay in her mind what Mrs. Peterson told her about the afterlife.

As the weeks went by Miracle started to warm up a little bit with the staff and the other kids at the group home. She even began walking to and from school with the other kids, sometimes.

One day, she was walking to school while reading a book and almost got hit by a car that was driving way over the speed limit. She looked

It's Never A Fair Game

up when she heard the voice of the person driving the car yelling at her to put the damn book down and watch where she was going. Miracle knew that voice way too well. The car was unfamiliar, but the voice would always be with her. It was James's voice. The hairs stood up on the back of her neck, and a chill ran through her body.

She wondered if he even knew or realized it was her he almost hit. The thought of him realizing it was her scared her. She decided it would be best to put her book up and hurry up and get to school. She still feared him, even though she no longer had any contact with him. Deep down she knew he was involved with her mother's death. She felt like either he had done it himself or knew who did it.

Sometimes she felt as if James would be coming to get her next. She knew just as much about him and his lifestyle as her mother did. Today was the first time she had seen him since he picked her mother up and never brought her back. Miracle knew James knew people and had connections, and if he really wanted her dead, he could have done it already. So maybe he wasn't out to get her. Either way, she wasn't taking any chances when it came to him and ran into the school building.

CHAPTER FOUR—A New Home

After school that day, Miracle thought it would be smart to walk home with the other kids. While walking home, she heard laughs and snickers coming from behind her. She kept walking, trying to ignore what seemed to be laughter about her. All of a sudden she tripped and fell. The laughter became even louder, and now it was confirmed that everyone was laughing at her.

Angela, one of the known mean girls in the foster care, walked up to her and said, "Sorry newbie. I guess you tripped over my foot." Marie, Angela's little sidekick, laughed uncontrollably at Miracle lying on the ground. The two girls stepped right over her and kept walking toward the foster home.

Miracle got up and started picking her stuff up from the ground. A voice from behind said, "Here you go. Are you all right?"

Miracle looked up to see who it was. It was Tiana. Tiana stayed in the room across from her at the foster home. Although they never talked, Tiana always smiled at her when passing her in the halls of the home. "I'm ok," answered Miracle. "Thank you for helping me."

"Oh, it's no problem. Angela and Marie ain't shit for tripping you up like that," she said. "Look, if there's one thing you need to know about fos-

It's Never A Fair Game

ter homes, it's that the kids here can be mean and ruthless for no reason at all. A lot of them come from broken homes and have been abused in ways you can't even imagine. So they treat others how they've been treated their whole lives."

"I understand," said Miracle.

"Look, just try not to be such a loner, ok? You make yourself an instant target."

Miracle appreciated all the advice Tiana was giving her, so she decided at that moment that Tiana was someone she should stick by. She seemed smart and knowledgeable. "I'm Miracle, by the way," she told Tiana.

"I know," she laughed. "Well, now that we have been formally introduced you're gonna stick with me, and I promise Angela and Marie won't be a problem anymore."

Miracle smiled, and the two continued the walk home, talking and getting to know one another.

From that day on they were inseparable. Tiana would come by Miracle's room every morning, and they would walk to and from school together. On the weekend they would always partner up in the group home activities. Tiana was 16, which was three years older than Miracle, so to her, she was like the big sister she

CHAPTER FOUR—A New Home

always wanted but never had. Having Tiana in her life now seemed to make the days, months, and years at the foster home go by faster.

Two years went by quickly. Miracle still thought of her mother often, but it seemed in a way that Tiana had unknowingly filled that void. She looked out for her, she taught her things about life, and she genuinely cared about her, just as her mother did. The only problem now was that Tiana would be turning 18 in a couple of weeks, and at the age of 18, she would be leaving her, just as her mother did. She knew she would be alone all over again. Miracle, without even realizing it began to act very distant toward Tiana, to the point where Tiana decided to get down to the bottom of this silent treatment and see what was wrong.

She went to Miracle's room one night and woke her up. "What's wrong with you lately?" she demanded to know.

"Huh?" A half-asleep Miracle wiped her eyes to find Tiana staring her in the face. "What do you mean?" she asked.

"I mean why are you being so cold and distant with me? Don't you realize my time here is winding down? I'm about to be 18 and kicked out on my ass, and my only real friend isn't even talking to me."

It's Never A Fair Game

"I'm sorry," said Miracle. "I don't mean to be distant, but when I'm sad about things that are beyond my control, that's what I do. I shut down."

"Oh, I see. Like when I first met you because you had just lost your mother, you wouldn't talk to people?"

"Yeah," answered Miracle.

"So what has you so down now?"

"You are leaving me," she said. "Since my mother died, you have been the only real friend I have had. And now, in just a couple of weeks, you will be gone, and I will have no one once again."

"Miracle, that's just not true," said Tiana. "I love you, and I will always be here for you, no matter what. I will come by and visit you here often, I promise."

This made her feel a little better, but Miracle still appeared to be very sad at the thought of only seeing her friend, sometimes.

"Don't look so sad still," said Tiana. "You haven't heard the best part yet."

"What's the best part?" she asked.

"When I turn 18 I will be an adult, Miracle! And as an adult, I'm able to go out, get a job, get a place to stay and even adopt a child from foster care if I want to."

"But why would you..." Miracle stopped herself in 'mid-sentence.

CHAPTER FOUR—A New Home

She quickly realized that child she was referring to must be her. "You could adopt me!" she shouted with joy. Miracle jumped up out of bed and gave Tiana the biggest hug.

Tiana smiled and replied, "That's right, Miracle. I can take you home with me. So don't be sad, friend. Our separation will only be for a short while. I will get a job, a place to stay, and then I will come for you, friend. That's a promise."

Two weeks went by fast. And Tiana was gone. Miracle seemed ok with it. She held on to what her friend had promised her. She knew it was only a matter of time before Tiana would start visiting her and eventually adopt her.

Chapter Five

WRONG PLACE, RIGHT TIME

Miracle seemed to be adjusting to living without Tiana every day, better than she expected. Maybe the fact that Tiana called her weekly made her feel like she was still there with her —well, somewhat. It was at night now that she mainly felt alone.

Since Tiana had been gone, her mother had been on her mind a lot more often. She could never accept not knowing who killed her mother. The police never found the killer. They just assumed it was a passerby who picked up a hooker and murdered her. Now, two years later, it was nothing but another cold case to them. But to Miracle, it was a mystery that one day she planned on figuring out. Not just who did it, but why they did it? And most importantly she wanted to find out James's involvement in the murder. Miracle knew he was responsible in one way or another, and she wanted to make sure her mother's death would not be in vain. She vowed that the person responsible would pay.

The next day was visitation day, and Miracle couldn't be more excited to see Tiana. She got dressed early and cleaned her room. Tiana always made fun of her when her room was messy. She wanted to show her that she was, in fact, maturing as a teenager and could keep her room clean. That way she would feel even better about her letting her live with her one day.

It's Never A Fair Game

Twelve o'clock came, and Tiana came strolling through the doors just like clockwork to see her friend. They gave each other a big hug and headed to Miracle's room to talk.

"So how have you been?" asked Tiana. "You been staying out of trouble?"

"Of course," said Miracle. "I've been thinking about my mom's death a lot lately since you've been gone, though."

"Thinking about it in what way?"

"Like how her murder was never solved...and how I think I know who's responsible for it...and how I plan on making them pay one day."

"Whoa there, Miracle. Pump your brakes," said Tiana. "I thought you told me the person responsible was supposed to be like this huge drug dealer?"

"He is," said Miracle. "But so? Karma has a bullet with his name on it as far as I'm concerned."

"Miracle, you don't know that he did it, though."

"Yes, I do. My heart and my mind have told me this since the day they told me my mother was found dead in that alley."

Tiana decided to leave that conversation alone and change the subject to lighten up the

CHAPTER FIVE—Wrong Place, Right Time

mood in the room. "Guess what," she said. "I have my first job interview next week!"

"That's great," said Miracle. "I'm so happy for you and proud of you."

"Thank you, sis," Tiana replied. "I'm doing this for us. I meant what I said, Miracle. I'm going to adopt you. It's just going to take some time to save money and get a place but getting a job is a good start, right?"

"You're right," said Miracle. "I can't wait for that day to come. It's going to be so great living together on our own."

"Yeah, it is," said Tiana. "But for now, Miracle, can you do me a favor?"

"What's that?" she asked. "Can you focus on continuing to make good grades in school and not so much about revenge on this drug dealer? He will get his, Miracle. Trust and believe, if he killed your mother, then it will eventually come to light. But for now you gotta focus on you, baby girl. Focus on your future and having a better life than your mother did. You're smarter than me when it comes to those books. A person like you should go to college after high school. And when I adopt you, I'm going to make sure you go."

Miracle promised Tiana she wouldn't focus on James and her mother's death so much,

It's Never A Fair Game

and instead, she would study more and keep her grades up. The hours flew by and before they knew it, visitation hours were over. Miracle walked her friend to the door and gave her a hug.

"Don't be sad; you know next visitation day I'll be back."

"Yeah, I know," said Miracle. "It's still a whole week away, though."

"Look, here's the phone number for where I'm staying. Call me anytime you need me. If I'm not there, just leave a message with Gina. She's the girl I've been staying with. She knows all about you and will be sure to give me the message. I'll always call you back as soon as I can."

"Thank you," said Miracle. "And good luck on that job interview."

"Thanks, friend," said Tiana and she walked away, headed to the bus stop.

Now that school was back in session, Miracle dreaded the walk to and from school without her best friend. The walk seemed so cold and lonely now. A lot of the other girls had boyfriends who picked them up from the group home and gave them rides to school but Miracle didn't. She had never dated anyone, and always felt shy around the opposite sex. Tiana, on the other hand, always had a boyfriend. But even when she had a boyfriend she always made time for Miracle.

CHAPTER FIVE—Wrong Place, Right Time

It was Miracle's sophomore year, and she would be turning 16 pretty soon. She had considered trying to appear to be interested in dating this year. She was probably one of the only girls her age who hadn't even kissed a boy. Furthermore, it would be nice, she thought, to have a male friend to escort her to and from school. But for now, she was a loner, once again.

Miracle tried to focus on the good things that were happening in her life. When she wasn't working, Tiana still came to see her every chance she got. She assured Miracle that she was saving every paycheck so she could get a place for them one day. In return, Miracle had been staying out of trouble and making the best grades possible. Miracle had also been looking into different colleges in the area to see what the qualifications and costs were to even go to college. Prices seemed ridiculous. There was no way she could ever afford anything like that, even with a scholarship, she thought to herself. But she had time to figure it out.

One day, while walking home from school, Miracle was startled by the sound of police sirens. They sounded like they were coming from a nearby neighborhood. Although sirens in that part of town were a familiar sound, it sounded

It's Never A Fair Game

like something big was going down. Miracle decided she needed to get home as quickly as possible, so she cut through some old abandoned houses to shorten her trip. As she passed through one of the houses, she noticed what seemed to be a bag sitting in a corner. She walked past the bag but then stopped. Her curiosity was getting the best of her. She couldn't help but wonder what could be in it. At the same time, she wondered if what was in it could harm her. Could it be a dead body chopped to pieces? *You just never know these days, she thought to herself. But she couldn't walk past it. She weighed her options on whether or not she should have a peek in the bag. Then she made the decision to look. She slowly unzipped the bag for just a peek.*

Whatever it was appeared to be green in color. She opened it all the way. She was at a loss for words at what she had found. It was money and lots of it. She couldn't be sure just how much it was, but she could tell it was hundreds of thousands.

Just as Miracle started to pick up the money she heard the sirens getting closer to her location. In addition to the sirens, she heard what appeared to be someone running. And it sounded like they were headed her way.

CHAPTER FIVE—Wrong Place, Right Time

Miracle decided to grab the bag of money and hide in the closet in the house until the sirens left. But the sound of running got closer and so did the sirens.

Before she knew it, a man ran into the house. He appeared to be looking for something. Instantly, she figured that he was looking for the bag. The man started to throw things around the house, angry that he could not find the bag. It was like he was so angry that he forgot that he was being chased. Miracle could only hope that the police got to the man before he got to her. She was sure he would start searching the room she was hiding in at any moment. Her heart was beating a million miles per hour. Sweat and fear consumed her.

The sirens were now louder than ever, and she could see the blue lights coming from the windows. She could hear the man cocking his gun and yelling at the cops. She knew that voice. It was James! Miracle was trapped in an abandoned house with James! She was sure he would find her hidden in the closet and kill her, just like he had killed her mother.

Miracle started to pray silently. *Mother, if you're watching over me like Mrs. Peterson said you are, can you please not let James find me? Please help me out of here, Mama.*

It's Never A Fair Game

It seemed only moments after Miracle said that prayer that James burst into the room she was hiding in and the police burst in after him. Feeling defeated, James dropped his weapon and got down on the floor as instructed. While lying on the floor, James noticed a bag in the closet and a girl holding it. Although she tried to hide her identity, it was no use. They locked eyes. He looked at her and mouthed her name silently. And just as soon as he did that the police were slapping the cuffs on him and dragging him out the front door.

Miracle thought this would be the perfect time to slip out of a window in the back of the house while the police were struggling to get James into the squad car. She grabbed the bag then quickly got out of the closet and headed to the back of the house. She opened the window, threw the bag out, and then hopped out after it. Miracle ran until she could no longer see any blue lights. Now she wondered what she should do. There was no way she could go to the foster home with a bag full of money. And there was no way she could continue walking the streets with it either.

Miracle called the only person she could trust. The only person who had been there for her since she had been at the foster home,

CHAPTER FIVE—Wrong Place, Right Time

Tiana. But when she called, Tiana didn't answer. Miracle left a message with Gina for Tiana to meet her at the park as soon as she could. Miracle went to the park and waited for Tiana.

About two hours later Tiana showed up, frantic. "Miracle, what's going on? Why aren't you at the foster home?" Tiana asked.

"Because I need your help," said Miracle.

"My help with what?" asked Tiana.

Miracle unzipped the bag full of money and showed it to Tiana.

Chapter Six

THE PLAN

"What is this and how did you get it?" Tiana demanded to know.

"It's money, and I took it from James," said Miracle.

"What? Are you crazy, Miracle? What do you mean you took it from James?"

"Well, I didn't exactly take it out of his hands or anything. I found it. It was stashed in an abandoned house. I was walking home from school and heard a lot of sirens coming in my direction, so I decided to cut through some old houses to get back to the home quicker. Well, while I was walking through one of the houses, I saw a black bag sitting in the corner of the floor. So I took it."

"How do you know it's James's money?" asked Tiana.

"I know because, before I could leave the house with the money I heard someone coming and hid in the closet. It was James, and he was looking for his bag. Luckily, before he could get to me hiding in the closet, the police came in and took him down. After they escorted him out of the house, I snuck out the back with the bag of money."

"So he never even saw you?" said Tiana.

"Well, I wouldn't say that. When the police took him down to the ground, he got a glimpse of me hiding in the closet."

"But you don't know for a fact that he saw you though."

It's Never A Fair Game

"We locked eyes, Tiana. He saw me. I know because he silently mouthed my name."

Tiana just stood there for a moment in disbelief at the story she had just been told. "So how much is it?" she asked.

"I don't know," answered Miracle, "but I'm willing to bet it's hundreds of thousands."

"We have to count it," said Tiana.

"But where? We need a plan," said Miracle.

"You're right, we do. But right now we need to get you to the foster home before the staff comes looking for you. It's getting pretty late. I'll take the money home with me and count it tonight when my roommate falls asleep. Tomorrow when you get out of school I'll be waiting for you so we can discuss the next move."

Miracle trusted Tiana, but she also knew that she had only known Tiana for two years. During the walk home, she was a little quiet, going back and forth in her mind on whether or not she should let Tiana take the money. But if she didn't, what was her alternative? Bringing it back to the home and it getting stolen from her or getting caught with it. Her back was against the wall, and she knew she would have no choice but to trust her friend and let her take the money back home with her.

By the time they made it to the home, Tiana

CHAPTER SIX—The Plan

could sense that Miracle seemed a little uneasy about the plan she had suggested. "Look, Miracle," she said. "Haven't I've always looked out for you and had your best interest at heart?"

"Yes, you have," said Miracle.

"Well then, you have to know that I would never do anything to hurt you or betray you. We're best friends, Miracle. If you didn't trust me you wouldn't have called me in the first place. You called me because you know you can trust me."

"You're right," said Miracle.

When Miracle and Tiana reached the foster home, they hugged and said their goodbyes until tomorrow.

That night Miracle lay in bed just thinking about the money and all the events of that day. She wondered how much was really in the bag. She knew whatever the amount was, it was definitely a life-changing amount. But why her, though? She wondered why she was the lucky one that came across the bag. It could've been anyone who found the bag in the house, but it was her. Maybe it was her mother, she thought. Maybe her mother was looking out for her all the way from heaven and guided her through that abandoned house that day so that she could find that bag and no one else. Miracle's mind was

It's Never A Fair Game

moving 100 miles per hour that night just thinking of all the endless possibilities that she could
use the money on. James was on her mind as
well, but for some reason, she felt in her heart
that with his track record of being a big-time
drug dealer for many years, this time he would
be going away for a pretty long time. The thought
of James in prison for a very long time made her
smile, and with that thought, she fell asleep.

The next day seemed to go by in slow mo-
tion. The school day seemed to be never-ending.
All she could think about was meeting up with
Tiana later that day. She was sure she had
counted the money by now, and she couldn't wait
to hear about the amount that was in the bag.
When the bell rang, she grabbed her book bag
and raced out of the school building as if she
was being chased. Once she got outside, her
nerves decided to kick in. *What if she doesn't
show? What if she's halfway out of the country
by now with my money?*

As soon as she started to believe her
thoughts could actually be a possibility, a voice
came up from behind and said, "Did you think I
had left town or something?"

She turned around to see Tiana standing
there with the bag of money. "Of course not," she
said. "I never once doubted you."

CHAPTER SIX—The Plan

Tiana gave Miracle a look of disbelief and then smiled. "Well, let's go. We have some things we need to talk about."

The girls walked to the park. They found an area where there were no other people around and plenty of trees to sit up against. They picked a tree and got down to business.

"Ok, so I can't take it any longer. How much money was in the bag, Tiana?"

Tiana looked at Miracle and said, "More than you could ever imagine."

"Tiana! How much? This is torture. I've been wondering all day long."

"Ok, ok, calm down, Miracle," laughed Tiana. "There is $500,000 in this bag, Miracle."

Miracle's mouth flew open. She had never seen more than a hundred dollars at once. "I can't believe we have $500,000," she said.

"I know," said Tiana. "But here's the thing, Miracle, we can't act like we have this much money even though we do. We can't go deposit a large amount of money like this in a bank account without it looking suspicious. The money is dirty."

"Dirty? What do you mean by dirty?" asked Miracle.

"Well, it's drug money. It's not money that we made from a legitimate job or business.

It's Never A Fair Game

That's why we can't deposit it. We have no way of proving we didn't steal this money from somewhere and no way of proving that we actually earned it. We have to play everything cool, Miracle. We have to go back to our normal lives, at least for a while. I mean, just a few months ago I was in the foster home just like you. There's absolutely no way I could have come up with this amount of money that fast by working a regular job paying me ten dollars an hour. I'll have to get an apartment for us, a car, have a little money in the bank but not enough for it to look suspicious. Once I get established then I can start the paperwork to adopt you. The courts should have no problem letting me adopt you because they will see that I can provide for us and give you a good, stable environment."

"So in the meantime, where will we hide the money?" asked Miracle.

"I'll put it a place no one would dare to look. I'll hide it in the backyard of my grandmother's house. She's in her 80s, and she doesn't get around that great. I wasn't allowed to live with her because she was considered to be too old.

The courts thought she wouldn't be able to properly care for me and keep me out of trouble. But that will be the perfect place, Miracle. No one ever goes there and especially not her

CHAPTER SIX—The Plan

backyard. The fact that I will be going there hiding the money and retrieving it won't look suspicious because I'm her granddaughter. I have a right to go see my grandmother, right?"

"Wow, Tiana. You really did go home and think everything through. It's as if I met you for a reason. It feel like you are the best thing that has happened to me since I lost my mother."

"Aww Miracle, you're my best friend as well. You're like the little sister I never had. I will always be here for you and look out for you. We're like family now. I really knew you felt the same about me when you called me to meet you about the money. I knew then that you trusted me with all that you had. When I took the money home that night I vowed to get you out of that foster home, make sure you go to college and have a great life. And you know what, Miracle? That's exactly what I'm going to do."

A teary-eyed Miracle hugged her friend. Miracle returned to the foster home that day feeling relieved and confident that everything was going to be alright. She now knew without a doubt that she could trust Tiana.

Weeks passed, and Tiana continued to make regular visits to visit Miracle. She would update her on the progress of the adoption. Miracle was pleased to know that her friend was living up to her word.

It's Never A Fair Game

Within the next six months, the judge ruled that Tiana could adopt Miracle. Miracle woke up the next day to find Tiana standing in her room with all of Miracle's stuff packed and ready to go.

"Tiana?" A half-awake/half-asleep Miracle rubbed her eyes. "What are you doing here so early? It's too early for visitation," said Miracle.

"Well, maybe I'm allowed to be here so early because I'm no longer a visitor."

Miracle gave her friend a puzzled and con-fused look. "So if you're not a visitor then what are you?"

Tiana smiled and said, "I'm yo mama now. The adoption was finalized yesterday. The courts are letting me take you home, Miracle. It's over." Miracle sprang up from her bed with tears of joy. Tiana had done everything that she told her she would do, and had successfully adopted her. She hugged her friend tightly. For a second it felt as if she was hugging her real mother. She had a flashback of how she used to give her mother the biggest hugs—the type of hugs that meant *'I love you more than anything in this world.' She hadn't been able to hug anyone like that since her mother's murder and it felt good to love someone like that again.*

Chapter Seven

JAMES GOES TO PRISON

After an excessively long trial, James was sentenced to 5 - 10 years on drug trafficking charges. His sentencing made the front page news. It read, "Drug Kingpin Gets Off Light" with a picture of James smiling as they took him out of the courtroom in handcuffs.

James knew with good behavior he could be out in three to five and the first thing on his to-do list would be to find Miracle, get his money back and kill her. James spent countless days and nights planning how he would make her pay for stealing from him. He knew as a kingpin he had the power to send his goons out looking for her and kill her while he was locked, up but this was personal. He wanted to handle this situation himself.

The days, weeks and months passed before James had his first visitor. To his surprise, it was his estranged son, Jamal. James and Jamal's mother never really got along as Jamal was growing up. She wasn't too fond of James's profession as a big-time drug kingpin. So she kept James out of her and Jamal's lives, but as time passed, he learned more about his father from people on the streets. When he would ask his mother about his dad, she always refused to give him any details as if she was scared he would go looking for him.

Once he became a teenager, he decided to stop asking questions and go out and find the

It's Never A Fair Game

answers. He was 15 when he met James for the first time, and to James's surprise, he didn't hate him. He didn't harbor any negative feelings for his father because he knew his mother was ultimately the reason why he never had a relationship with his father. Jamal began a relationship with James behind his mother's back and kept it from her for years. By the time she found out Jamal was visiting his dad regularly, it was only a few months before his eighteenth birthday; so it was pointless to try and keep them away from each other.

Now Jamal was 19 and visiting his dad in prison. As he walked up to the prison, he could feel the knots forming in his throat. He didn't know how his dad might react to him visiting him in prison. James walked into the visitation room and took a seat.

"Hey, Dad. How you been?"

"I'm doing all right, son," said James. "I've just been lifting weights to pass this time. What brings you to see me?"

"Well, you are my father," said Jamal. "I just wanted to make sure that you were doing ok and that you didn't need me for anything."

"Need you for anything like what?" laughed James.

Jamal leaned in and whispered, "Like the family business."

CHAPTER SEVEN—James Goes To Prison

James's eyes opened wide. "Boy, you don't know anything about the business. And you can thank yo ol' square-ass mama for that."

Jamal held his head down as if he were ashamed. "But Dad, I'm a grown-ass man now. My mama no longer makes my decisions for me. She doesn't know I'm here. And...if she did I wouldn't give a damn."

"Boy, watch it now," scolded James. "I know you harbor a little bit of anger toward your mama for keeping you away from me, but she only wanted the best for you. This street life ain't for everyone. Motherfuckas get killed all day every day out there, and she just didn't want you to be one of them, and I can't say I blame her for that."

"But Dad, I'm smart. I'm mature, and I have the book sense and the street sense now, thanks to the few years we did get to spend to-gether. Just tell me what you need me to do. I'll do anything to prove to you that I can live up to my family name in this business."

James quietly sat as if pondering some-thing. "Well, there is one little problem that I could use your help in solving."

"Oh yeah, what's that?" asked Jamal eagerly.

"Well, when a nigga got busted in the

It's Never A Fair Game

abandoned house I left my drug money in the house. The police found the drugs but never found the money."

"So, do you want me to go look in the house for the money then?" asked Jamal.

"No, no, son, I already know it's not there anymore. In fact, I know who has it. As the police took me down to the ground, I got a glimpse of a familiar face hiding in the closet holding my motherfucking money."

"Well, who has it?" asked Jamal.

"Miracle," he said. "Miracle Johnson has my money, and I want it back. I used to date her ol' crackhead ass mama years ago. Her mama ended up getting murdered tricking out there in the streets and Miracle got sent to a foster home. I hadn't seen her since. I'm not even sure that she's still there. If she ain't 18 already, she should be turning 18 soon."

"So what exactly do you want me to do, Pop?"

"I need you to find Miracle. When you find her I want you to befriend her. This girl isn't a dummy. You will have to earn her trust before she may ever tell you about my money and where it's at. And when she does, I want you to get my money and take the bitch out. If you can do that, I'll give you half of whatever's left in the

CHAPTER SEVEN—James Goes To Prison

bag. Listen to me good now, boy," said James. "Don't step into some shit that you can't get yourself out of now. If you ain't up for the job then decline right now, lil nigga."

Jamal looked into his father's eyes and said sternly, "I got this. I won't let you down."

"Good. Now my lawyers are working on my case. They found a few technicalities with the way the police department handled some evidence so I may be getting out a lot sooner than expected. When I get out, I expect this little situation to be handled and to have my money waiting on me. You do that, and I promise you I will show you the ropes of the family business and make you a very rich man."

"I promise I won't let you down, Pops." Jamal shook his dad's hand and got up from the table.

As he turned to walk toward the door, James yelled, "And tell ya mama, I said hey." James let out a loud laugh, and Jamal continued out the prison door. Once outside he took in a deep breath of the fresh air.

"I have to do this," he repeated to himself. "There's no turning back now." He got into his car and drove off.

Chapter Eight

LOVE AT FIRST SIGHT

"Get up, Miracle, or you're gonna be late for your own graduation," yelled Tiana.

It was finally the big day. Miracle had been living in a generous-sized apartment with Tiana for the past six months, and things had been going great. After the adoption was final she moved in with Tiana and she became her legal guardian. Although they were friends, Tiana did her best to be a mother figure for Miracle.

Tiana went into Miracle's room to make sure she was out of the bed. "Girl, if you don't get out of that bed—you walk across the stage in two hours!"

"I know, I know," said Miracle. "I'm getting up right now."

Miracle got dressed, and she and Tiana made their way to the graduation. On the way there Miracle seemed quiet and distant.

"What's up your butt?" asked Tiana. "You should be happy today and extremely proud of yourself for graduating."

"I am proud of myself," said Miracle. "But I can't say I'm 100% happy. I wish my mom were here to see me walk across the stage because it would have made her happy, T."

Tiana pulled the car over. "Miracle, your mother is happy. Don't you know that when our loved ones pass they're still with us? They become angels that watch over us. Your mother is always watching and smiling down from heaven

It's Never A Fair Game

at what a smart and fine young lady you have turned out to be, despite everything that you've been in through in life. Against all odds, you're graduating. She's not just happy, baby girl, she's ecstatic. And so am I," said Tiana.

Miracle looked up and smiled as if she were smiling at her mom in heaven.

"Now let's get to this school before they call your name, and you're not missing crazy girl," Tiana laughed.

Miracle laughed at her friend too. She always knew the right things to say to pick her up when she was feeling down. She convinced herself that Tiana was an angel sent down by her mother to love her as she did.

The weeks after graduation flew by. Miracle didn't have a job, and Tiana stayed on her back about getting her college applications filled out. Tiana wanted Miracle to succeed in life by all means necessary.

"Miracle," yelled Tiana, "I'm on my way to work. Please get at least two applications done today, ma'am. I'm going to check when I get home." she laughed.

"Ugh, you act like such a mom," said Miracle. "But ok, since you won't let me get a job..." Miracle rolled her eyes.

"Miracle, all I want you to do is focus on

CHAPTER EIGHT—Love At First Sight

school. I work, and we have a nice little stash hidden in my granny's backyard, in case you forgot," she said.

"No, I haven't forgotten," said Miracle. "It's just...I get bored."

"Well get on Facebook and make some friends," she laughed. "I have to go. I'm running late."

"Okay, bye T," yelled Miracle.

Tiana left for work and Miracle decided to create a Facebook page. Miracle never had many friends, nor did she have any social media accounts. She made a page and then anxiously waited for the requests to come. Within the first hour, Miracle had fifty friends. She was amazed at how quickly social media worked. Before she knew it, she found herself playing around with Facebook for hours, looking at other people's pages and adding a couple of pictures to her profile. The college applications slipped her mind once she entered the world of social media.

She decided she had played with Facebook enough for the day and was about to log off when she received another request. It was from a male named Jamal. He looked cute and clean-cut. Miracle decided to accept his friend request. Not even thirty seconds later she noticed she

It's Never A Fair Game

had a direct message from him. This was all new to her, and she was very hesitant about having a one-on-one conversation with a stranger she'd never met before. But when she read the message, there was something about the way he spoke to her that made her want to reply. He said, "I just wanted to tell you that you are a very beautiful girl with a very unique name."

The message made her smile, and she decided to write back. "Thank you." Before she knew it, she and Jamal had been messaging for two hours. She realized Tiana would be home soon and she had yet to finish two college applications. She told Jamal she had to go and that she enjoyed his conversation. He agreed and decided to shoot his shot and ask for her telephone number. Although hesitant, Miracle decided that she wouldn't mind talking to him again and she gave him her cell phone number.

As the days and weeks went by Jamal quickly became a part of her daily routine. She would awake every day with a "good morning, beautiful" text message from Jamal. Throughout the day they would talk to each other about everything. They began to form a friendship that Miracle had never had with anyone outside of Tiana, and she took notice.

"Hey Miracle, what's up with you and this

CHAPTER EIGHT—Love At First Sight

Jamal boy that you're always talking to?"

"He's a just a friend I met on Facebook," said Miracle.

"Well, you sure talk to him a lot for him to be just a Facebook friend."

"Well, I like him, if that's what you're asking me."

Tiana rolled her eyes and made a comment under her breath.

"What was that, T? I know you said something," said Miracle. "T, are you jealous?"

Tiana looked at Miracle sharply. "Now why in the hell would I be jealous? Girl, please. If anything, I'm just concerned about you spending so much time talking to strange men that you meet on Facebook."

"Not strange men, Tiana. Jamal is one person, and I think you shouldn't judge him before you get to know him. He's a cool guy. As a matter of fact, he wants to hang out this weekend. I asked him to come by the house before we go out so you can meet him personally. How does that sound, T?"

Do I have a choice?" she asked.

"No," laughed Miracle.

The weekend came fast, and although she and Jamal had talked for weeks, she was nervous about meeting him.

It's Never A Fair Game

When he arrived, Miracle answered the door to find a tall, dark-skinned, handsome man smiling at her. He looked even better in person than in his pictures. He was clean-cut and shaved, with a smile to light up anyone's day. His style was impeccable, and her attraction to him was almost immediate.

"Well hello, sweet thang," he said. "You look beautiful, but I wasn't expecting anything less than that anyway."

Miracle laughed. "Jamal, you're a mess. But thank you. You look very nice yourself. Come in. I would like you to meet my friend, roommate, and foster mom Tiana. Tiana, he's here," yelled Miracle. "Come and meet Jamal."

Tiana walked into the living room to meet Jamal.

"Well hello," said Jamal. "Wow, what are the chances that I find two gorgeous ladies living under the same roof? I'm Jamal."

Tiana shook his hand. "Nice to meet you, Jamal," she said. "That's very sweet of you to say. So sit down. Tell me a little about yourself. How old are you, Jamal?"

"I'm 19," he said.

"Oh ok, are you from here?"

"Yes, actually. I was born and raised here. I grew up mostly with my mom. My dad ran the

CHAPTER EIGHT—Love At First Sight

streets, and she didn't allow me to have a relationship with him. I guess she wanted to keep me as far away from that lifestyle as possible," he explained.

"Oh ok, well, that's not a bad thing that she did that. It's hard out here in the streets, especially for young men. So do you have a relationship with your dad now?"

"Uh, no. Not at all," stuttered Jamal. "I guess I didn't feel I needed one now that I'm an adult.

Tiana gave Jamal a side-eye glance as if she questioned his response. "Oh ok," she answered. "Jamal, do you mind if we step outside so I could have a word with you?"

"Sure," he said.

"T, what is this about?" asked Miracle.

"Miracle, calm down. I just want to have a word with Jamal one on one. Nothing really serious, so get your panties out of a wad and calm down," she chuckled. She walked outside and Jamal followed behind her.

"So what's up?" he asked.

"Look, Jamal, I'm just gonna cut straight to the point. Miracle is like my little sister—better yet like my child. You see, I don't know if she told you this or not, but we were in foster care together. I got out before her, got my life together, and adopted her.

It's Never A Fair Game

I'm telling you all of this because I want you to know and understand how much she means to me. Fucking with her is like fucking with me so don't do it."

Jamal looked a straight-faced Tiana in the eyes and muttered, "I got ya."

"Good," said Tiana. "We shouldn't have any problems then."

Miracle came to the door. "Are Y'all done talking? Because I'm ready to go."

"Yeah, we're done," said Tiana. "Now y'all go ahead and have a good time."

Miracle and Jamal headed off.

Miracle began seeing Jamal regularly. Either he was always hanging around the house, or they were going places having fun. Miracle had never dated anyone before, so this was a whole new experience for her, and she loved every minute of it. Jamal was a real romantic and affectionate type of guy. He opened doors for her; he held her hand when they went places. Sometimes, he just seemed too good to be true, this is how Tiana felt about him.

She expressed to Miracle that she felt Jamal was too good to be true and that he might be hiding certain parts of his life. But Miracle didn't care, honestly. All she cared about was how he made her feel.

Chapter Nine

A NIGHT TO REMEMBER

That night Jamal told her to get dressed up. He told her he would be taking her somewhere special. She straightened her hair and polished her nails. She never really wore makeup, but tonight she put on makeup. As she got dressed, she tried to imagine where they might be going and what he might have planned. Jamal was so spontaneous it was hard to know what he was thinking, thought Miracle.

She wanted for the first time in her life to get sexy for someone and for that someone to be him. For the first time she felt physically attracted to someone. It wasn't until she met Jamal that being a virgin seemed like a bad thing to her. Since she met Jamal thoughts of losing her virginity to him crossed her mind quite often. She feared what he might say and think if he knew that she was a virgin. Would he laugh, or would my virginity not be an issue? She felt certain that tonight might be the night she lost her virginity because they would be spending some alone time.

All of her thoughts came to an abrupt halt when she heard the doorbell ring. "Tiana," she yelled, "I'm not quite finished getting ready. Can you let Jamal in?"

"I guess," said Tiana. Tiana went to the door and let in Jamal. He was dressed very nicely. His hair was freshly cut and he smelled of men's Ferragamo cologne. "Well, you look nice," she said. 'What's the occasion?"

It's Never A Fair Game

"Occasion?" he asked. "There isn't one, really. I just wanted to take Miracle on a special date."

"Oh, ok. Well, that's sweet of you. She should be ready in a second. You can have a seat, Jamal, and I'll go see how much longer she will be."

"Ok, that's cool." Jamal sat down and set his phone on the coffee table.

Tiana went to check on Miracle. She walked into Miracle's room. "You ready yet, girlie? Jamal's out there looking clean and smelling really nice for you," she grinned.

"Tiana, stop it."

"What?" asked Tiana. "I'm just saying, that man is dressed up as if he has some major plans for you, girl."

Miracle blushed but at the same time felt a bit nervous. "Tiana, I don't know if you know this or not, but I'm still a virgin," said Miracle. "If to-night goes really well and everything feels right, then I'm thinking about losing my virginity to Ja-mal."

"Well," Tiana said, "you're a grown woman, and I'm not going to tell you whether or not to do something you want to do. But what I will tell you is that once it's gone, you can't get it back. So you need to make sure that he's special enough to

CHAPTER NINE—A Night To Remember

you if you decide to lie down with him. And if so make sure you protect yourself. You're going to college in the fall, ma'am, so no babies allowed," she laughed.

Miracle laughed back. "Ok Mom," she joked. She walked into the living room to find Jamal sitting on the couch waiting for her. Tiana had been right. He looked very handsome. "Hey Jamal," she said. "I'm ready."

"No, he said, "you're beautiful is what you are."

She blushed and hugged him. Her nose immediately got filled with the scent of a sophisticated and elegant man. His cologne smelled of an aromatic woody fragrance, and she felt as if she could be happy hugging him and smelling him all day long.

"You ready to go? he asked.

"Yes, I'm ready," said Miracle. "See you later, Tiana. Don't wait up," laughed Miracle.

The two left and drove off. Tiana closed the door and walked into the living room. She sat on the sofa and noticed that Jamal had left his cell phone on the coffee table. She walked over and picked it up. "Oh well," she said. "I guess he can get it whenever he drops Miracle back off at home."

As she started to lay the phone back down,

It's Never A Fair Game

it began ringing. Something in her told her to answer his phone. She knew it was wrong, but there was a piece of her that deep down didn't trust Jamal and thought he's just too good to be true. And with all those lingering thoughts, she decided to answer his phone. She picked it up but didn't say hello. Immediately she heard an automated system come on and say, "You have a collect call from (a voice said "James, your dad"), an inmate at the Atlanta correctional facility. Do you accept the charges?"

"Yes," Tiana answered.

James got connected to the line. "Jamal, have you handled that bitch Miracle yet? I'm getting out real soon, boy, and I need my money as soon as I get out."

Tiana couldn't believe what she was hearing. A piece of her wanted to hang up on him, but without even realizing it she responded, "This ain't Jamal. And on everything I love, you will not see a dime of that money and Jamal won't lay a finger on Miracle."

Before he could say another word, Tiana hung up in James's face. It all made sense now. Jamal felt too good to be true because he was. This whole thing was a set-up. He never planned on being this knight in shining armor to Miracle. *He's James's son, and he's looking for the*

CHAPTER NINE—A Night To Remember

money and using Miracle to get to it, she thought. "Oh my God," she said. "I have to try and warn Miracle before she gives this creep her virginity. Or better yet, tells this fool anything about the money and her past."

Tiana raced to her phone to try and call Miracle. But Miracle's phone went straight to voicemail.

"All right, keep those eyes closed until I tell you to open them," said Jamal.

"Ok," said Miracle. "But are we almost there yet?"

"Yes, we're pulling up right now."

They pulled up to a tall building. It was a hotel that had a restaurant at the top of it.

"This is absolutely beautiful, Jamal. But why are we here?"

"Well, there's this cool restaurant at the top of this hotel that spins while you're inside eating there. And the best part about it is that you get the best view of the city. All the lights and colors are just breathtaking. Just like you are," he said.

Miracle smiled and kissed Jamal. The softness of his lips made the kiss sweet and sensual. *So far, so good,* she thought to herself. They rode the elevator up to the restaurant that overlooked the city holding hands.

It's Never A Fair Game

"Wow, this is beyond amazing," she said. "Thank you, Jamal."

"No, thank you," he said, "for allowing me to bring you here."

Jamal always knew the right things to say, and at the right times. He just made her feel so wanted and loved. They had an amazingly romantic dinner.

"I have another surprise for you," said Jamal.

"This dinner at this restaurant was everything. What could be better than this?"

"Well, I was able to get a hotel room here for the night, if you would like to stay. I don't want to rush you into anything, but I figured you might want to stay and hang out here a little longer."

"Jamal, I would love to," she said. "This place is amazing. And you—well, you're amazing too."

Jamal smiled. For a minute it all felt real, not like just a scheme or plan anymore. His feelings for Miracle felt genuine.

As they approached the room, Jamal once again told Miracle to close her eyes. She closed her eyes as instructed. Jamal took her by the hand and walked her into the room. "You can open your eyes now," he said.

When she opened her eyes, she saw a

CHAPTER NINE—A Night To Remember

candle-lit room with romantic red LED lights all around the ceiling. The room smelled like strawberries from the scented candles. Soft music played in the background.

"Oh my God, Jamal, I've never seen anything as beautiful. How did you do all this?" she asked. "And how did you know that I would agree to come to the room?"

"Well, let's just say I was rolling off faith that you would say yes," he laughed. "And I have ways of getting things done." He winked. "But I'm very happy that you agreed to join me. And just so you know, we don't have to do anything if you don't want to. We can just talk and sleep if you want to. I'm good as long as I'm with you."

At that moment she knew that she wanted to have sex with Jamal. He had officially won her over. She turned to Jamal, looked him in his eyes and said, "I'm here because I want to be with you. And whatever happens tonight, trust and believe I want it to."

Jamal leaned forward and gave Miracle a kiss. She kissed him back. He grabbed her by her waist and pulled her body up close against his. She felt soft, and he all of a sudden felt hard. She could feel him. It was a feeling that she had never felt before. But she liked it. He took her hand and placed it on his penis. She looked up at

It's Never A Fair Game

him with frightened eyes.

"What's that look for?" he asked. "Are you a virgin?"

Miracle's face flushed. "Why would you ask me that?" she stuttered.

"You just seem a little nervous," he said. "I mean, it's no big deal if you are. That's a good thing to me."

Miracle looked surprised by his response. "Well, I'm actually glad that you feel that way," she said. "I've never been with anyone before so yeah, I am still a virgin."

"Baby, that's nothing to be ashamed of. Just follow my lead." He put Miracle's hand back on his penis and had her rubbing it and stroking it. He gently kissed her on the neck while unzipping the back of her dress. Her dress hit the floor, and he walked her over to the bed. He picked her up and laid her down softly. He told her to unzip his pants as he unbuttoned his shirt.

Miracle did as she was told. This was all new to her, and it felt exciting. Once his pants and shirt were off, he laid Miracle back down and kissed her passionately on her lips. His kiss was so sweet and passionate that the feeling of another person's tongue in her mouth didn't even gross her out, she thought to herself.

Jamal went from kissing her lips to kiss-

CHAPTER NINE—A Night To Remember

ing her all the way down her chest and in between her breasts. He lifted her bra up and began to lick on and around her areolas. This tick-
led her, and she giggled a little. He moved down,
kissing her stomach area. He kept kissing her
all the way down her stomach to her panties.
Miracle looked uncertain about what he was doing.

He looked up at Miracle's face and asked
her, "Do you trust me?"

"Yes," she answered. "Why?"

"Because you look scared," he said. "But if
you trust me then just know that I would never
do anything to hurt you. I only want to make you
feel good and make you happy."

She leaned forward and kissed Jamal on
the forehead. "Well, make me feel good, then,"
she said.

And with that, he pulled her panties down
and licked her in between her legs. He licked her
in circles and in a million different motions. The
more he licked on her clitoris, the more she felt
herself leaking. Miracle had never felt anything
like that before. Within seconds she found herself making noises that she had never made before. At times she felt embarrassed at the
sounds she was making. But then again it felt so
damn good she didn't care who heard her.

It's Never A Fair Game

He came back up and pulled his under-wear down. Miracle gasped. She had never seen a penis in person before. And although she had never seen one before, she was pretty sure he was big for his size. He looked at her face and saw that she was scared; he told her to get under the covers, and then joined her. He got on top of her then kissed her slowly and passionately to ease her mind. He took the tip of his penis and rubbed it against her clitoris. This made Miracle squirm with pleasure. He could feel her getting very wet. He continued to stimulate her clitoris with his penis until she moaned uncontrollably. He penetrated her vagina and made love to her slowly.

This is it, Miracle thought. *I can't get this back.*

That night she experienced emotions and feelings that she had never felt before. She was glad that she never lost her virginity to anyone other than Jamal. It felt like he was made just for her.

The next day she woke up in Jamal's arms. Miracle felt like she was falling in love. Now she needed to know if Jamal felt the same way. And if he did feel the same way, she needed to know if he would still love her after finding out about her past. She never told Jamal about her

CHAPTER NINE— A Night To Remember

mother's death, how she grew up or about the money. She felt that he had always been so open and honest with her and now she felt she needed to do the same with him.

"Jamal, are you awake?" she asked.

"Yes baby, I'm awake. Is everything ok?"

"Yeah, I just need to talk to you about some things."

"Ok. What up?" he asked.

"Well, I have feelings for you that I've never had for anyone else before. Jamal, I'm not really sure what being in love feels like, but I think I may be falling in love with you. I guess I'm wondering if you feel the same way about me."

"Miracle, he said, "I don't go all out for every woman I meet. Only women I see a future with. I can see that with you. You are genuine, loving, smart and funny. You're everything a man could ask for. So to answer your question, yes, I'm falling in love with you too."

Miracle smiled and kissed Jamal. He had said everything that she needed to hear to tell him about her past.

"Well, now that I know our feelings are mutual there are a few things about my past that I think you should know about.

"Ok," said Jamal. "But there isn't anything you can tell me that could keep me away from

It's Never A Fair Game

my baby. Well, unless you're a killer or some shit. Then I got to bounce," he joked.

"No silly, she said. "But I do want to tell you about my past. My mother was a struggling addict for years. She even had me while still on drugs. I was thrown into foster care as a baby, but my mother got her life back together, and the courts gave me back to her. We lived a happy life for a while. But my mother ended up dating a drug dealer and relapsing on his drugs. Shortly after that, she was found murdered. I was only 13 years old, and her death devastated me. I tried so hard to get her to leave her boyfriend James, but she wouldn't do it. After that, I got sent right back to foster care. That's where I met Tiana. She looked out for me like I was her little sister. She's always been there for me since I had no one else. She even adopted me when she got out of foster care."

"Wow!" said Jamal. "I never would've guessed that you had been through so much pain and heartache in your life. And after all of that, you're still so strong."

"I had no choice but to grow up fast and trust that God did everything for a reason. Somehow it feels that my mom drops unexpected gifts and blessings on me from time to time she laughed. Like Tiana, and you maybe?"

CHAPTER NINE— A Night To Remember

Jamal grinned and gave Miracle a big kiss. "I can believe that," he said.

"She also dropped a blessing on me a couple of years ago that I've never told anyone other than T about."

"Well, you can trust me, baby. I would never repeat anything that you didn't want to be repeated," said Jamal.

"Well, a couple of years ago, before Tiana adopted me, I was walking home from school, and I cut through an old abandoned house. As I was walking through the house, I saw a duffle bag. I opened the bag, and there was money in it. All of a sudden I heard voices and a lot of commotion. I got scared and hid in the closet. The next thing I knew, I heard the voice of James, my mom's ex, in the house looking for the money I had just found. I just knew he would kill me if he found me in that closet holding his money. But the next thing I knew the police burst into the house and took James away. The police never even saw me. The only problem is that James got a glimpse of me sitting in the closet holding his bag. I took the money and I ran. Tiana and I have been using this money to make better lives for ourselves. I know if and when James gets out of prison I'm going to be the first person he's looking for. And Tiana knows this as well. Look,

It's Never A Fair Game

Jamal, I'm only telling you about this because I love you and I wouldn't want anything to happen to you because of something I did in my past."

Jamal sat there as if he was shocked by Miracle's story. "Well, I thank you for giving me that heads-up. And so you know, nothing's going to happen to me or you and no, I'm not leaving you alone because of what you told me. That still ain't enough to make me walk away from you, girl," he laughed. "I do have one question, though. What did y'all do with the money that was left?"

"We have it hidden," she said. "I vowed to Tiana that we would never discuss where it's hidden with anyone else."

"Oh, ok, I understand that," he said. "Well, your past is the past for a reason. From now on let's just focus on our future," he said.

Miracle smiled and laid her head on Jamal's chest. Jamal lay back in the bed and rubbed Miracle's back. It was supposed to all be simple, but now he found himself falling in love. But *what do you do when only one person can have your loyalty? He didn't even want to think about it. He just wanted to enjoy the moment with Miracle while he could.*

Chapter Ten

THE TRUTH SHALL SET YOU FREE

Miracle and Jamal spent the whole weekend together at the Westin hotel. She loved every minute of being with him. He was loving and easy to talk to, and she almost hated to go home. A part of that was because she knew she would have to hear Tiana's mouth about not calling and checking in with her the whole weekend. She was sure Tiana had been probably trying to call her, which is why she kept her phone off the entire weekend. She wanted to make sure the final decision of whether or not she should sleep with Jamal was hers and not based on anything Tiana said. Now the weekend had come to an end, and she needed to explain to Tiana why she hadn't contacted her all weekend. Jamal dropped Miracle off at home and headed home himself.

"I'm home. Tiana, where are you, girl? I have a lot of tea to spill."

Tiana came out of her bedroom holding Jamal's phone in her hand. "Well, don't spill your tea just yet. You may want to sip mine first," she said sarcastically.

"What's this all about, T? And what are you doing with my man's phone?"

"Oh, so he's your man now? Hmmph, that's funny," said Tiana.

"And what's so funny about him being my man? Could it be the fact that I have one and you don't, and you're jealous?"

"Not no, but hell no," said Tiana.

It's Never A Fair Game

"Maybe it's the fact that you don't even know who the hell your man really is."

"And what makes you think I don't know who my man is, T?"

"Well, let's just say if you knew then you probably wouldn't have spent the whole week-end with him, ignoring me."

"Ok T, enough of this bullshit; just tell me what you know, or what you think you know."

"Oh baby girl, I don't think I know, I know. You're sleeping with the enemy. Jamal is James's son. The same James who killed your mother and the same James whose money you stole. Jamal doesn't give a damn about you. He's only using you to get to the money for James."

"How do you know this?" asked Miracle.

Tiana threw Jamal's phone on the table. "As soon as y'all left that night I realized Jamal had left his phone on the coffee table. I picked it up, and it rang. I decided to answer it. I don't know why, but I did. When I answered it, it was a collect call from James from prison. He specifi-cally said "your dad James." The most chilling part about it was he asked if Jamal had taken you out yet because he was getting out soon and will need his money when he does. At that point, I let him know I wasn't Jamal and that he would-n't be touching you or that money and hung up."

CHAPTER TEN—The Truth Shall Set You Free

Miracle stood there in disbelief. After having such a great weekend with Jamal, she didn't want to believe anything that Tiana was telling her. But somehow, deep down she knew it was true.

"Miracle, I know you like him, but you're going to have to confront him. You need to let him know that you know who he is and what he's up to. And after that, we need to get the hell out of this city. James said that he will be getting out soon based on some legal technicality. Miracle, I refuse to let anything happen to you. We have to make some moves and do it quickly."

"I understand," said Miracle. She realized she couldn't argue with Tiana even if she wanted to. She was right. She would have to let Jamal go, and she would have to leave the city before James could come looking for her and the money.

The next day Jamal showed up unannounced. He rang the doorbell. Tiana looked out the peephole then went to get Miracle. "He's here, Miracle. You know what you have to do."

"Yeah, I know," she said. Miracle went to the door.

"Hey baby," he said. "Do you know I spent all weekend with you and it wasn't until this morning when I got ready to text you that I real-

It's Never A Fair Game

ized that I must've left my phone over here the night I picked you up. Girl, you must really have my head gone," he snickered.

Miracle just stood there looking at him with a straight face.

"What's wrong, baby? Why are you looking so serious?"

"Well, what's wrong is that I trusted you, Jamal, and you lied to me. I told you all about me, my life and all I went through. But you have never been honest with me."

"Ok baby, what in the hell are you talking about? I'm completely lost," he said.

"This is what I'm talking about." Miracle threw Jamal's phone at him. "You left your phone here all weekend, and Tiana answered one of your phone calls. It was from James, your dad, from prison. He was wondering had you taken me out yet. And he said he was going to need the money when he got out. This whole thing has been a set-up from the beginning. You found me on Facebook so you could do your dad's dirty work." Miracle found herself on the verge of tears. "I feel so fucking stupid. You even knew all about the damn money before I told you about it, and you played me like you didn't know shit. I thought you really loved me." She burst into tears. The betrayal seemed too much for her

CHAPTER TEN—The Truth Shall Set You Free

heart, and the tears began to flow down her cheeks.

"Miracle, I'm sorry," said Jamal. "You're right. I am James's son. And in the beginning, I found you so I could get his money back. I grew up with my mother. I never had a relationship with James until I was a teenager. When he got locked up, I just wanted to continue a relationship with him. I just wanted to show him that I could be the son that he never knew I could be. Loyal. But when I took the job, I never thought you would be such a beautiful person inside and out. I never thought I would fall so hard for you. I didn't tell you who my dad was, but I meant every word of how I feel about you. I promise, Miracle, I'm not going to let anything happen to you."

"How are you going to stop him?" asked Miracle.

"Tiana said that James will be getting out soon based on some legal technicality."

"Damn, I didn't know that," said Jamal.

"And another thing you didn't know is that James killed my mother. When I was thirteen, and my mom was dating James, he got locked up on some drug charges. My mother relapsed on his drugs while holding them for him. When James got out, he beat my mother for using his drugs and made her work in the streets as a

It's Never A Fair Game

prostitute to get his money back. One night my mother never came home. I know James set her up to be killed that night. I just know it."

Now Jamal stood there in horror. All these years he wanted to be a part of his father's life he never knew his dad was a murderer. "Miracle, I didn't know any of that when I agreed to find you for my dad. And yes, he asked me to take you out but I never planned on killing you. I was going to get you to tell me where the money was and just disappear. But now that I've fallen for you and I know the truth about James, I have to protect you from him. If my father was responsible for killing the woman he loved, I know he will kill her child."

"I don't know, Jamal. You betrayed me. How can I trust you after you kept all of those secrets from me?"

"I don't know, Miracle. But I hope you can find it in your heart to let me love you and to let me help you. Just give me a few days to go see James. I'll call the whole thing off. I'll tell him that he needs to find someone else to do his dirty work. Then by the time they release his evil ass, you and Tiana can be long gone with the money."

"And what about you?" she asked.

But right now I need to find out when James is scheduled to be released. We need to know how much time we have."

CHAPTER TEN—The Truth Shall Set You Free

"Okay, she said. "And I need to go in the house and have a talk with Tiana."

The two hugged goodbye and Jamal left to see what he could find out.

After a lot of explaining and convincing, Miracle finally got Tiana on board with trusting Jamal and going with his plan. They both thought it would be a good idea to keep a packed bag in the trunk of the car. They needed to stay ready at all times. They knew what James was capable of and at any given moment Jamal could be telling them that James was headed their way.

Chapter Eleven

JAMES' REVENGE

The next day Jamal texted Miracle to let her know that he was on the way to the prison to see James. He said after leaving the prison, he would call and tell her what he found out. When Jamal got to the prison, he was immediately informed James had been released that morning. He instantly felt a lump in his throat and his heart drop. He had no idea where James might be. But he knew he had to get to Miracle and warn her that James had been released. He texted Miracle and asked her to meet him at the park in twenty minutes. He didn't want to take the chance of being followed to Miracle's house by one of James's goons. She texted back *ok and let Tiana know she would be back as soon as she met up with Jamal to find out what was going on with James. Tiana hugged her friend and told her to be careful.*

It didn't take long for word to get out on the street that James was out. He made his presence known immediately to his old drug corners. He put the word out that he needed to know where his son Jamal was and where Miracle lived. The same day he got out he had Jamal and Miracle's addresses and had planned on paying them both a visit. He decided to start with Jamal. He hadn't been answering his calls, and he felt it was time he found out why. James and his goons drove to Jamal's house. They kicked in his door to find his house empty.

It's Never A Fair Game

"I guess he must be booed up with my damn enemy," he said. "Well, I'm about to go break that shit up. Phil, drive me to that bitch's house. We gon' pop a cap in both of they asses, get my money, and leave."

James was a man of his word. When he put it in his mind that someone had to die, he meant it. Betrayal was the worst thing a person could do in his book. Loretta had betrayed him when she took his drugs, and she paid for it with her life. Now if Jamal had betrayed him for that bitch who stole his money, then he would have to die too.

They pulled up to Miracle's house to find a car home. "Phil, you go around the back," said James. "I'm gonna knock on the front door." James walked up to the door and knocked.

Tiana came to the peephole and looked out. She had never seen that man before. "Who is it?" she asked.

"I'm Luther. A friend of Miracle's. Is she home?"

"Uh, I don't think Miracle knows anyone by the name of Luther, and I'm sorry, she's not here anyway if she did, so goodbye," said Tiana.

This angered James. "Bitch, I think you better open that door and let me have a word with you before I let myself in."

CHAPTER ELEVEN—James' Revenge

This scared Tiana. She didn't know who this unknown man was at the door, but she had a gut feeling it was James. She backed away from the door and ran to her room to grab her phone but as soon as she turned around Phil was already in the house with her phone in his hand.

"You looking for this?" he asked. He grabbed Tiana and walked toward the front door to let James into the house.

James came in and took a seat. "Now you see, bitch, that's all you had to do in the first damn place. Now I'm sure you're wondering, who I am and what I want. Just like I'm wondering who the hell you are because you don't seem to be the thieving little heffa I'm looking for. I'm James, and you are?"

"I'm Tiana. Miracle's friend and roommate. Why are you here? What do you want?" she asked.

"Bitch don't play with me," yelled James. "You know what I want. I want my motherfucking money. As a matter of fact, you're the same little bitch that answered Jamal's phone that day, aren't you? Yeah, I know it was you. Well, guess what? You don't have all of that mouth now, I see. So this is how it's going to go down. You're going to tell me where my money is or you're going to die. So what's it gonna be?" asked James.

It's Never A Fair Game

Tiana looked James in his eyes and whispered, "Go to hell."

James stood up and got in Tiana's face. "You'll get there before me. Phil, take this trick out of my face and handle that for me. I'll be waiting out in the car."

James walked outside and closed the door behind him. He could hear Tiana's screams as he walked toward the car.

Minutes later Phil walked outside and got into the car. "Where to now, boss?" he asked.

"Take me to see my disloyal-ass son," said James.

"Sure thing," said Phil.

When they got to Jamal's house, James noticed that Jamal's car still wasn't in the driveway. "Looks like he isn't home, Boss," said Phil.

"Well, that's ok," said James. "We're just gonna go in anyway and make ourselves at home until he gets here. I want to surprise him, anyway. As a matter of fact, Phil, park the car down the street, so he won't even know he has company when he arrives."

"Okay, Boss," said Phil. Phil kicked the side door in and let James into the house. He then moved the car down the street so Jamal wouldn't know anyone was at his house when he arrived. Miracle arrived at the park and sent Jamal

CHAPTER ELEVEN—James' Revenge

a text that read, "I'm at the park; where are you?"

He responded, "Outside your car window."

Miracle looked up to see Jamal standing outside her window. "Well, get in the car, then," she scolded.

"Ok, ok," he said.

"Now tell me what you found out when you went to visit James today. Was he pissed when you told him that you weren't going to go through with his plan anymore?"

"He still doesn't know," said Jamal.

"Why Jamal? Why wouldn't you tell him?"

"I couldn't tell him because they had already released him, Miracle. He was gone before I even got there."

"So what does this mean?" she asked.

"It means that he's looking for us. He's going to want his money, and he's going to want revenge. We have to watch our backs, Miracle, and we have to get the hell out of town real quick, like tonight quick."

"So what's the plan?" she asked.

"Well, I was thinking on the way over here that once we leave the park, I'll go home and pack a few things then meet you and Tiana at the house. From there we pick up the money and head straight out of Atlanta."

"We pick up the money?" she asked.

It's Never A Fair Game

"Look Miracle, I don't want any of the money. All I want to do is make sure you make it out safe from James and his goons. After that, you and Tiana can take the money and never see me again if that's what you want. But I'm hoping that won't be what you want."

"Miracle leaned forward and gave Jamal a kiss. "Of course that's not what I want," she said. "I love you, Jamal."

He smiled and kissed her back. "I love you too, Miracle. But now we have to hurry before it's too late."

Miracle agreed, and they hugged and parted ways. The drive back to the house seemed as if it took longer than usual. Miracle found herself speeding trying to get to Tiana to let her know that James was out. She decided to call Tiana's phone to warn her if any unfamiliar face came to the door not to answer it, but Tiana wouldn't answer the phone. She tried calling her three times, and each time it rang all the way out and went to voicemail.

"Shit," said Miracle. "She's probably asleep or in the shower."

A few minutes later she pulled up at home. She raced to the door to find that it wasn't locked. Miracle immediately knew that something wasn't right. She pulled her mace out of her purse and walked into the house. She didn't have to walk far before she found Tiana's lifeless body lying on the floor. "Tiana," she yelled.

She ran over to her body and picked her head up. She wasn't breathing. There was a pillow lying on the floor next to her body. Miracle concluded that she had been suffocated. She held her friend and cried. "Tiana, I'm sorry. This is all my fault. If I had never taken that money none of this would have happened." She cried and cried at the loss of her friend. Tiana was the best thing to happen to her after her mother's death, and now she was dead too. Miracle knew who was responsible for this. It had to be James.

She raced to her phone and called 911. When the police and paramedics arrived Miracle was adamant that she knew who was responsible for her friend's death, and she insisted that they go find James immediately.

"Miracle, I'm Detective Thurman. I know this is a tough time for you and believe me, we're going to get the person who did this to your friend. But I'm going to need you to come to the station with me and answer a few questions."

Even though she already knew who the killer was, Miracle agreed to go to the police station to answer some questions. She spent countless hours trying to tell the police that

It's Never A Fair Game

James was responsible for Tiana's death but without any proof, they couldn't go charge him with anything.

"Ssshh Phil. I think I heard someone pull up," said James. He looked out the window and saw Jamal in the driveway. "Yeah, that's his monkey ass. Phil, stand behind the door in case he tries to run when he sees me," instructed James.

"Okay, Boss."

Jamal stuck his key in the front door and walked into the house. He cut the light on to find James sitting on his couch. "Dad," he said. "When did you get out?"

"Today," said James. "But for a person who doesn't know I'm out, you sure don't look surprised to see me."

"I'm very surprised," said Jamal. "Why didn't you tell me that they were letting you out early?" he asked. "I would've thrown you a party or something."

"A party?" laughed James. "Well, I called you this past weekend. You didn't answer my call. As a matter of fact, Tiana, Miracle's roommate, answered it. And you know what she said?"

"No Pop, what did she say?"

"Well son, she said that I wasn't gonna see a dime of my money.

CHAPTER ELEVEN—James' Revenge

Now I don't know what would make a bitch assume something like that, but I know one thing."

"What's that, Pop?"

"Her assuming days are over if you know what I mean." James looked over at Phil, and they both laughed.

Jamal didn't dare ask what happened to Tiana. He knew she was dead. "So you only got to Tiana?" asked Jamal.

"Yeah," said James. "You were the mother-fucker that was supposed to be handling Miracle. But from what I hear in these streets she's still running around here, not only still breathing, but still breathing with my money. That's a problem, Jamal. And when I have a problem, I deal with it."

"Yeah, I heard," said Jamal. "Miracle told me how you dealt with her mom. I always thought Mom kept me away from you because you were a dope dealer. But now I know the truth. Mom wanted me to stay away from your ass because you're a killer. How could you kill a woman you loved?"

"Fuck her," yelled James. "That bitch wasn't loyal. It's a fine line between love and loyalty. You can't love a bitch that's unloyal, so she had to go." James stood up and pulled his gun out of his

It's Never A Fair Game

coat pocket and pointed it at Jamal. "I loved you too, son. But you're an disloyal little nigga. I was ready to show you the ropes of the family business. I was ready to make you my right-hand man. But you couldn't do one thing I asked you to. Kill that bitch and get me my money back. So now, because you used your heart instead of your head, you ain't nothing to me."

"So that's it, Dad? You just gonna kill me, just like that?" asked Jamal.

James pulled the trigger and shot Jamal in the chest. "Yep just like that," he said. "Let's ride, Phil."

James and Phil left Jamal bleeding in the middle of his living room floor and set out to find Miracle.

Chapter Twelve

MIRACLE'S HAD ENOUGH

After she spent hours in the police station telling the police everything she knew about James, the police let Miracle go. She couldn't go back to the house. She knew James would be watching the house. She decided to go by Jamal's and let him know what happened to Tiana and that they would need to be leaving tonight.

Miracle drove to Jamal's house. She saw his car in the driveway and knocked on the door. After a few minutes, no one came to the door. She knocked again and waited, but once again no one came to the door. Miracle could feel her heart racing. Something didn't feel right. She decided to walk around to the side door. When she got around to the side door, she saw that it had been kicked in.

She frantically ran into the house to find Jamal lying in a pool of blood, but he was alive. "Jamal, oh my God, what happened? Who did this to you?"

"James did it," he muttered. "It was James."

"I'm going to call 911, baby, just stay with me." Miracle called 911. "Please," she screamed.

"Please save my boyfriend. He's been shot in the chest, and he's bleeding everywhere."

Miracle hung up with the 911 operator and cradled him in her arms. "Please don't die, Jamal. James killed my mother and Tiana. I can't lose you too. Please baby, just hold on," she pleaded.

It's Never A Fair Game

Within the next 10 minutes, paramedics arrived on the scene to take Jamal to the hospital. Shortly afterward the police arrived, and to their surprise Miracle was at yet another crime scene that night. "Ms. Johnson, we meet again," said Detective Thurman.

"Yeah, unfortunately. But it's because y'all didn't believe me when I said James was trying to kill me. He killed Tiana when he couldn't get to me and now he's shot Jamal, his own son because Jamal was trying to help me get away from him."

"Well, the real question is why does he want to kill you, Miracle?" asked detective Thurman. "Why is this man after you? Is there anything that you haven't told us?"

Miracle sat quietly, contemplating whether or not she should tell the police about her taking James's money. "Well, a long time ago he dated my mom. After my mom's death, I got sent to foster care. James lost some money, and he thinks I'm the one who took it. So he's after me for this money he thinks I stole."

Detective Thurman turned and looked Miracle in her eyes. "Well, did you take his money?" he asked.

"I-I-I did," she stuttered. "But it's all gone now."

CHAPTER TWELVE—Miracle's Had Enough

"Well, we're not going to let him harm you whether you still have the money or not. That's not justification for killing anyone."

"But he is," said Miracle. "And it started with my mother. He killed my mother for stealing drugs from him. James is a killer."

Detective Thurman turned to a now teary-eyed Miracle. "Well, if what you say about James is true, then we need to get him off these streets as soon as possible, and we need to get you somewhere safe."

"What if I can help you catch him? What if I wear a wire and get him to confess to the murders? Would that work?" she asked.

"Well, yes, it would work and be helpful but with a man that dangerous, I'm not sure if I want to put you in harm's way like that," said Detective Thurman.

"I know, but I can do it," said Miracle. "I can get him to say what you need to hear so you can charge him for these crimes. Please, just give me a chance. If it seems like the plan isn't working y'all can take over at that moment, but you at least have to let me try. I owe it to my mom and Tiana for what he's done to them."

"I'm sorry, Miracle, said Detective Thurman. "I just can't let you go up against a man that vicious. We'll figure out another way. But in the

It's Never A Fair Game

meantime, we need to get you safe."

"Don't worry about it. I'll protect myself."

"Well, at least take my card," said detective Thurman. "Call me if you think of anything else you haven't told me or if you need anything."

An angry Miracle stormed off and drove away. "Put a detail on her," said Detective Thurman. "Bodies are dropping all around that girl. I don't want her body to be next."

She drove to a nearby hotel and checked in for the night. That night all she could think about was Tiana. James had successfully taken away everyone she loved and everyone who loved her. There was just no way she could let him get away with this, she thought. She would have to handle James all on her own, without the help of the police.

She got up early the next morning and went to the pawn shop. She decided that she needed to get some protection. She bought a .22 caliber pistol and a small handheld voice recorder and went back to her hotel.

She realized she needed to come up with a plan. She decided to go to the corners where James sold his drugs and put the word out that she was looking for him. She told random people on the streets to let James know if he wanted her, he could find her at the old aban-

CHAPTER TWELVE—Miracle's Had Enough

doned house where he got arrested, in two hours.

Once Miracle put the word out, she went straight to Tiana's grandmother's house to retrieve the money from the backyard where they buried it years ago. They would go retrieve money from the stash when they needed it, but they never removed the entire bag. This time Miracle was taking it all. She dug up the money and threw it in the trunk of her car. She drove back to the hotel with the money.

I need to come up with a plan, she thought. I cannot let James kill me or take this money away from me. She decided she would take the money out of its original bag and refill it with the things from her luggage. She then placed the money in her suitcase. She headed over to the abandoned house an hour earlier than the time she was supposed to be there. She arrived with the gun in one coat pocket and the recorder in the other. This is it, she thought. She decided to say a prayer before she walked into the house. Mom, Tiana, if y'all are listening I'm going to need your help today. I just ask that you ladies continue to watch over me like you always have. This is for you.

Miracle got out of the car and slowly approached the abandoned house. She walked in,

It's Never A Fair Game

and to her surprise, James was already there.

"James, what are you doing here so early?" she asked.

"Well hell, I could ask you the same thing," he said.

"Are you alone?" asked Miracle.

"Yeah, I'm alone. I don't need no help to handle you, baby girl. I wanted to have all the fun of taking you out by myself."

Miracle reached in her pocket and slid the recorder on. "Taking me out? So you want to kill me like you did my mother and Tiana, huh?"

"Hahaha. You got it all wrong, baby girl. See, I didn't kill your mama. She killed herself when she used my product. I loved your mama. But she was unloyal. And once you show me that you can't be trusted, then ya ass has to go. Because I once loved your mama I let someone else have all the fun of taking her out," he laughed.

"But what about Tiana?"

"Oh, you mean your rude-ass little roommate? Nah, I didn't kill that bitch either. I let my partner handle that. But you and my pussy whipped son, y'all's asses were all mine. If he had just done what the hell I told him to do, you and I wouldn't even be standing here today. But no, he fell in love and couldn't do it. So now I have to do the shit myself. Did you really think I was going to let you get away with taking my money?" asked James.

"I don't know," said Miracle. She began stepping back toward the front door with her hand in her pocket and on the trigger as James walked closer to her.

"What are you backing up for?" asked James. "We haven't even started this party yet."

"What party?" asked Miracle. "There isn't going to be any party. Not for you anyway," she said.

"Oh, I'm gonna party alright. Just as soon as you hand over my bag of money and I send you home to your mama." James pulled his pistol from the back of his pants. "Now hand me my money," he demanded.

Miracle extended her arm to give James the bag and shot him through her jacket pocket. The impact made her fall to the ground as well. She looked up and saw James lying on his back, shot in the chest. Miracle got up and took his gun away. To her surprise, she heard police sirens. She grabbed the bag of clothes and ran out the back door with the pistols. By the time she got to her car, she could see officers running into the abandoned house with guns drawn.

It's Never A Fair Game

Miracle cranked up her car and slowly drove away from the crime scene. She called Detective Thurman and asked him to meet her at the park. When he got there, he found Miracle sitting on a park bench crying.

"Miracle, what's wrong? Did something happen?"

"Yes," she said. "I got him. I got him before he got me." She pulled out the two guns and gave them to the detective.

"I'm confused," he said. "What did you do, Miracle? What happened?"

Miracle reached into her other pocket and hit play on the tape recorder. When the tape finished playing, he looked at Miracle and said, "I'm sorry. I'm sorry you had to go through all of this. But I'm happy that it's finally all over and that you can finally move on with your life. Did you kill him?" he asked.

"I don't know," said Miracle. "I heard police sirens, and I ran."

"I had a police detail following you. He probably called for backup when he heard the shot. Here, give me all the evidence, and I'll handle it from here." Detective Thurman hugged Miracle and took the guns and tape recorder out of her hands.

CHAPTER TWELVE—Miracle's Had Enough

"Detective, do you happen to know how Jamal is doing? I haven't been able to get to the hospital to check on him."

"He's doing pretty well, actually," he said. "He fought hard to stay alive, and after his surgery, he's up talking and doing fine. Why don't you go see him?" said Detective Thurman.

"I will," said Miracle. "I will, right now."

The two hugged and parted ways. Miracle headed to the hospital and Detective Thurman went to the abandoned house.

Miracle walked into Jamal's room to find him asleep. She sat in a chair by his bed and just watched him sleep. *Thank you, Mom, she said as she looked up at the ceiling. In a sense, she felt her mom had made sure Jamal survived so that she would always have someone looking out for her and wouldn't be alone.*

Jamal heard Miracle's voice and opened his eyes. "Thank you, God," he said. "She's still by my side."

Miracle jumped up and gave Jamal a big hug. "Why wouldn't I still be by your side? You turned on James for me. You love me, and I love you." She leaned forward and gave Jamal a kiss. "Look, I do have to get out of town for a while, but I promise I'll be back for you," she said.

"Why?" asked Jamal.

It's Never A Fair Game

"Because I shot James," she said. "It's over baby."

"Is he dead?" he asked.

"I'm not sure, but I shot him. But even if he doesn't die, the police now have enough evidence to charge him with my mother's murder, Tiana's murder and your attempted murder. We're going to be ok now, Jamal."

They hugged each other. "Baby, I will be back to check on you in a few days, but right now I have to get out of this city before James's goons come looking for me."

She kissed Jamal and left the hospital as quickly as she could. For the first time, Miracle felt relieved. She felt she had gotten justice for her mother. This made her smile. "*So where to now?*" she asked herself. *Florida. I could really use a little sun and a beach. She laughed. She had never been to a beach before. I guess it's time to live a little, she thought. Miracle got in the car with her luggage full of money and headed down the highway.*

Jamal lay in his hospital bed half asleep when he heard the nurses rush a bed by his room door with someone named James who had been shot in the chest. He was pretty sure that was his dad. He waited a few hours and asked a nurse if someone by the name of James

CHAPTER TWELVE—Miracle's Had Enough

was admitted with a gunshot wound. The nurse told him yes. "Did he survive?" asked Jamal.

"Yes," the nurse said. "Why do you ask?"

"Oh, I think I know him, and I am just curious," said Jamal. "Can you tell me what room number he's in so I can call his room and check on him?

"He's in room 112," said the nurse.

"Oh, ok, thank you," said Jamal. Jamal waited a few hours until the nurses over him changed shifts. He then mustered up the energy to put on his clothes and ride a wheelchair down to James's room. He stood over him for a while, just looking in the face of a man who tried to kill him.

James opened his eyes to see Jamal standing there. He had tubes in his mouth and could not speak. "Remember me?" said Jamal. "Your son. The disloyal motherfucker that you tried to kill. Well, guess what, Dad? I didn't die. And neither did Miracle. But after all the hurt you caused that girl, it's only right that you die. You were right about one thing, Pop. I'm a very disloyal motherfucker, especially to a man who tried to kill me."

Jamal picked up a pillow and placed it over James's face. He held the pillow down with all of his strength.

It's Never A Fair Game

James tried to scream, but his screams were muffled by the tubes in his mouth. Jamal held the pillow over his father's face until he no longer heard any sounds coming from his father's mouth. Jamal suffocated James to death.

He then rolled out of his room in his wheelchair and back to his bed as if nothing ever happened. He undressed and got back into his hospital bed. He sent Miracle a text that read, "I love you, baby!" with a smiley face.

She texted back immediately, "I love you too, baby."

He smiled and muttered under his breath, "I love you until I get this money from you." Jamal laughed and drifted off to sleep.

TO BE CONTINUED...

THANK YOU...

I just want to give a special thank you to my kids, family, friends and everyone that believed in me and encouraged me to step out on faith to get the book done. Also, I'd like to give a special thank you to Mr. Armani Valentino for taking on my project and turning my dream into a reality.

Autographed copies available at
www.JessicaKPowell.com

www.ingramcontent.com/pod-product-compliance
Lightning Source LLC
Chambersburg PA
CBHW051837020726
47502CB00005B/1823

* 9 7 8 1 9 4 4 1 1 0 3 7 6 *